LANDS AND FORESTS

ANDREW FORBES

Invisible Publishing
Halifax & Picton

Library and Archives Canada Cataloguing in Publication

Title: Lands and forests / Andrew Forbes.

Names: Forbes, Andrew, 1976- author.

Description: Short stories.

Identifiers:
Canadiana (print) 2019007969X | Canadiana (ebook) 20190079703
ISBN 9781988784250 (softcover) | ISBN 9781988784311 (HTML)

Classification: LCC PS8611.O7213 L36 2019 | DDC C813/.6—dc23

Edited by Bryan Ibeas
Cover and interior design by Megan Fildes | Typeset in Laurentian
With thanks to type designer Rod McDonald

Printed and bound in Canada

Invisible Publishing | Halifax & Picton
www.invisiblepublishing.com

We acknowledge the support of the Canada Council for the Arts, which last year invested $20.1 million in writing and publishing throughout Canada.

Canada Council
for the Arts

Conseil des Arts
du Canada

ONTARIO ARTS COUNCIL
CONSEIL DES ARTS DE L'ONTARIO

an Ontario government agency
un organisme du gouvernement de l'Ontario

for CC

INUNDATION DAY

THEY BEGAN MOVING the houses in 1954. Those too large to be moved they would set alight, as the families and their neighbours gathered to watch.

Believe me when I say that it was a burdensome thing to live in a condemned town, a place soon to cease its existence. That every casual act carries an urgency, a fire, when your home's destruction is a foreordained event.

"They're doing it for electricity, Holland," my employer, Lester Smart, said to me one lunch hour as I stood outside the dairy's garage. "Electricity and cars. The Americans are after all that Labrador iron. Ford and GM, I mean. And where they're concerned, you can bet Ottawa will bend over backwards to accommodate."

"It stinks pretty bad," said Robert Lacey, who was having a cigarette. Lacey was a bit of a drunk, but he held himself together well enough to be a decent worker. We had known each other in school and spoke from time to time, increasingly about the changes to our home, which was all anyone seemed able to talk about for months.

"I'm told they call it *progress*, Robert, and it's only the fool and sentimentalist who oppose it," said Smart. "I guess we'll just have to wait and see what it brings us."

And that was it: the waiting. Waiting and watching and being unable to see beyond that fixed date. Trying to picture tens of thousands of acres of flooded land—to imagine cemeteries, where your family has lain for generations, lost under thirty feet of moving water. In your dreams maybe you could picture the park you played in as a child suddenly being at the bottom of a river, the church you attended being skimmed over by a massive freighter, but likely you couldn't. I certainly could not. The human imagination, it seems to me, cannot easily conjure such things. And so we could only wait to see just what our world would look like.

I thought I might leave this place altogether. I had a brother in Ottawa. My uncle Roger was in Toronto, a shop supervisor for the Transit Commission.

Something would come along, I felt, some new direction would come into or be granted to my life, though I'd no concrete notion of what that might be. I would hope people would see me as capable of a good many things. That would be a word I would like to hear applied to me: *capable*. Not mediocre, not average, but capable, in the best sense. That I could do several things, and teach myself to do what I did not already know. I flatter myself, perhaps, but it is not true to say that all men possess capability. My father, as an example, had patience and sense, but lacked ability. Whereas I had all three, enough to run a small engine repair business on the side.

Anyway, there were possibilities.

Poppy Sturges's husband, Alex, was known to be a good man. Before he died, he was liked in all corners of Loucksville, trusted in all dealings. It was generally held that he ran a good farm. Calamity struck, though, when he'd gotten his arm caught in a thresher during the harvest, and by the time they got him to Cornwall, he'd lost too much blood and there was nothing to do but call Poppy.

Poppy came to work in the office several months later. Smart had been a friend of Alex's, and he told Poppy, shortly after the funeral, that he'd be happy to help her out any way he could. So she filed, answered the telephone, followed up on accounts. She was an excellent worker, I was told, beavering away in the thin-walled office with the slat blinds always closed, per Lester Smart's preference.

I would see her there in the office, a quiet presence, slipping in the door, sitting behind a hulking metal desk, or moving toward a bank of green file cabinets, her arms full of papers. She seldom spoke, at least in my company. Though I did my best to be polite, I will admit that I did not fully conceive of her as an individual in those days. It would be more correct to say that I saw her as a fixture: an aspect of the place, of Mr. Smart's office, and the business conducted there.

It was a Tuesday in September, 1957. I'd just finished my early-morning run around Loucksville and the surrounding towns, and was once again checking the truck's oil. That was a habit of mine, almost a dictum: keep it ready. Meaning the truck, but also other things. Be ready. Think ahead.

Smart approached me as I stood wiping my hands with a rag. A great round man whose nose whistled when he breathed, he said, "Holland, I wonder if you wouldn't mind doing something for me."

"Of course, Mr. Smart," I said, "what is it?"

"I'm sending Poppy Sturges into the bank with a deposit, and I don't think she ought to be alone with so much cash. I wonder if you'd drive her. You can take my car, if you wish."

Minutes later, Poppy and I were in Smart's gleaming black Chevrolet Bel Air, exchanging pleasantries on the two-lane toward town.

I sat at the wheel, in uniform. Smart didn't ask me to wear a uniform, but I did anyway. It gave me a straighter back. The cash box sat in the middle of the sedan's front bench seat, a way station along the great distance of runnelled blue vinyl between us. And on the other side was the woman, I was sure, with whom I would soon be in love.

I mean you to know that: I knew right away.

She was luminous in a way I don't think you would understand if you were not there next to her on the wide bench, with the sun streaming through her hair. Her widowhood had worked to make her more tangible, made it appear that she had lived more in this world, been present for more of the things that mattered. I felt a charge that I hoped she felt, too. In her bones, in the skin of her face. The wind buffeted the car and the sun glinted off its hood and into my eyes, and I felt it all, saw us both crystallized inside the moment, preserved within a great, hard clarity.

I had nowhere to put these feelings.

She was, I thought it right to assume, committed to being a widowed mother, to doing what she could to provide a life for her little girl. That she was done with romantic love and all the rituals. But I felt what I felt. You may rightly call it love. And like a rising tide or a wall of water, there seemed little point in trying to stop it.

Like most of us, Poppy was scared and anxious about the completion of the seaway. But in the main, she was hopeful. She was hopeful that such progress, writ so large—heavy machines literally altering geography—would necessarily impose some small bit of the modern world on this place.

Most others in the doomed towns and villages feared that very thing, but Poppy knew the world she wanted to leave behind. That world chewed the arms off good men and left women and their children alone. She hoped the modern world would be a little different.

Her home, which stood on high ground, would be spared. But most of the town, and the other towns along the river, too, would soon be moved. Buildings would be lifted and relocated or razed, their replacements built on a piece of land selected by the government's engineers, and then suddenly, Loucksville would be to the north and east of the old farm and the Sturges house. We had trouble fathoming it, though the work was well underway.

An entire town, moved. How could it be the same place?

My house, where I lived alone, was a bungalow in a small development off the highway, farther out of town. It would be underwater in a few months' time. I had accepted the government's money, slight as the sum seemed. There weren't likely to be any better offers.

One evening, on a chill November night, Poppy Sturges stopped in. I suppose I had pointed it out to her as we passed on our way into town in Smart's Chevy.

At just past six, with the sun gone and the grass bleached and dry and ready for winter, she swung the nose of her old Pontiac off the highway and onto the crescent where my bungalow lay. I imagined Poppy was just stopping to say hello, as she pulled in at the end of the drive and stepped out. Maybe she felt it was the right thing to do, having seen the door of my garage open and me, clad in coveralls, lit garishly, tinkering away at greasy things inside. Perhaps, with her town soon to become a historical footnote, she felt emboldened. I cannot say for certain just what drove her actions. That is for her alone to say.

"Hello, you," I said, squinting into the dark, discerning her identity. Poppy was in a skirt and thick stockings, a long coat, a scarf around her neck. "What brings you by?"

I believe I had a smile on my face.

"Just happened by, I suppose," she said. Then she turned back to her car, opened the door, and retrieved a little girl of four or five in a thick coat and a wool hat. "This is Evey," Poppy said, looking down at her daughter.

The child had long limbs and almost translucent skin. Her pale eyes peeked out beneath red bangs.

"Well, hello," I said. "Happy to meet you, miss."

Evey smiled, then retreated behind her mother's legs.

I would raise her as my own, I said to myself.

"What do you do here?" Poppy asked, nodding toward the garage.

"Nothing worthwhile," I said, and though it was not a nice place, and it did not show me to any advantageous effect, I led them inside. There was a bare bulb hanging from the beams. The air smelled of oil and damp concrete and faintly of sweat. The uneven floor seemed to radiate cool air, while the plywood walls pulsed with old moisture. There were tools arranged in rows, hanging on the pegboard behind a broad work table. There were large clamps and tins of oil. A calendar with a picture of a Cadillac on it.

"You repair things?" she asked.

"If they need fixing, yes, I try."

"Do you take money for your trouble?"

"On occasion," I said. "It depends on the job."

"There's a sump pump in my basement's stopped working," she said. "Do you think I could ask you to take a look at it? I could pay you something."

"I wouldn't take a penny," I said. "Can I come by this weekend?"

"Saturday afternoon would be perfect," she said. She took a nubby little pencil from a coffee tin on my workbench, leaned over the greasy and beaten wooden work surface, and etched her address on Saturday's date, just below the Cadillac, though I knew very well where the Sturges farm was. Then she strapped Evey back in her Pontiac and got in herself, saying, "I'll see you tomorrow at work."

I watched her go, tail lights swallowed by November's dark, before heading back into the shop. I stood there for a time holding a wrench, turning it over in my palm. Then I shed my coveralls, closed the rolling door, switched off the light, and went into the house.

Their visit had left me buzzing, weak-kneed. I paced about the living room, then decided I needed air, so I slipped on a coat and stepped out into the night, felt the chill wind race up my sleeves and across my face.

I walked across the highway and into a field, frozen grass underfoot.

I looked at the sky, which held no answers.

Poppy has said that she and Alex had been very much in love—and yet, as in most marriages, they could also be utterly monstrous toward one another. After six years, they had both developed a sort of mithridatic callousness. Each reserved their deepest cruelties for the one they could not live without. It reflected a lack of imagination, an inability to picture their lives without the other, and so they withheld no barb, feeling certain each would stand and absorb the abuses.

Then Alex had gone and died, and in the immediate aftermath, there came several days when Poppy was sure she would die also. But Evey was there, and that forbade it. And so Poppy had had to invent a new way of living.

In addition to taking a job, she had the farm parcelled. Poppy sold lots around the house, ninety-eight acres of good pasture and grain land. She auctioned the farm equipment, including the thresher that had taken Alex's arm.

But buyers were few, and those few were wary. Land values, since the start of the project, had been significantly depressed, and most of Alex's equipment was outdated, good for little more than parts. With what she made off the sale of the land and the equipment, she was able to pay for the funeral and a few outstanding debts, but little else.

Still, she kept the house, and three and a half acres around it.

"For Evey to play on," she said.

On the Saturday of my visit, Poppy's apron was bright yellow. Her hair, once blond, was browner now, but still fair, and tied back into a ponytail but for a few strands about her ears and temples. She wore denim pants and a tan work shirt, rolled to the elbows. She was the picture of everything you could ever hope to see waiting for you at the door. Her face framed by thin lace curtains as she turned her head and called to Evey somewhere inside.

The house was empty-seeming, its siding's light blue paint fading. Poppy opened the door at the side, off the kitchen, and walked in her tall rubber boots out to the lane where I had parked. The afternoon was bright and large-skied. The slanting November sunlight made the fields appear endless.

Inside she led me, Evey in her arms, to the dank cellar. At the bottom of the damp sump hole sat the hulking, rusted pump.

"I don't need it now," she said, "but I will come spring. I hope you can fix it."

I unclamped its hose and hauled the pump out of the hole and looked it over. Rusty water seeped onto my pant leg and across the earthen floor. "Might be best if I just take it home and look at it there," I said. I carried it out the cellar door and heaved it into the trunk of my car.

Back upstairs she made tea. We sat at the kitchen table talking while Evey played with a set of blocks near our feet. The house was modest and I felt immediately comfortable in it. Light flooded the kitchen, golden and sharp. Poppy spooned honey into her tea. I was disarmed by her assuredness.

"I should probably be going and leave you alone," I eventually said.

"Not at all," she said. "You're welcome to stay. I just have to..." She looked at Evey, then at the clock on the wall. "I'm sorry. I'm not sure what I'm trying to say. Evey needs to nap. Can you stay until I get her down?"

"I'll be right here," I said.

Poppy took the child in her arms and walked out of the kitchen and through the parlour. I heard her climb the stairs, then in a few moments, the faint sound of her voice, singing.

This is where I want to be, I thought. *Here and nowhere else.*

When Poppy re-emerged a half-hour later, my teacup was empty and I was sitting silently at the table with my hands folded, listening to the silence of the house.

"I'm sorry to have taken so long," she said. "You shouldn't have waited. I'm sure you have things to do. I just wanted to walk you out to your car."

"No, it's fine," I said. "That would be fine."

As we stood next to my blue Dodge, she took my hand and, with absolute certainty, she leaned to my cheek and kissed it.

"That. That is what I meant to say earlier," she said.

What I came to know about Poppy was her great capacity for sadness. In the mid-evening dark, once Evey had gone down, we would pad about the unlit house, sombre, while the radio sang distantly. It was not simply that she was still in mourning for her husband. It was something more— something in her bones. It was in her downcast eyes, a vacancy that was not even remotely related to vacuity. It was in that same spot where most people held happiness like a trophy on a shelf. She was quick to smile, but the smile would soon thin, trail off, become something different.

We spent evenings and weekends in one another's company. It was never in question. We had found one another. The propriety of it seemed never to have entered her mind, but if I'm being honest, I had some pause. I was not quick to suggest, for example, that we dine outside the house. I preferred that we stay in. I preferred that we keep it to ourselves. I wanted there to be nothing to spoil what we'd found, the small flame we'd kindled.

We were chaste through that winter, but in spring, just as the lilac came into blossom, she said to me, "I think we should. I want to." And I stayed the night. We were quiet, careful not to wake Evey, who slept in the small room adjacent.

I woke early the next morning. I have always been an early riser. I lay awake and still in the ringing silence of the house, thinking. Poppy, her eyes fluttering, lay on her side, facing me. Birds called.

In three weeks the water would rise. How would it change us?

My house was already gone: smooth, chalky earth lay where it had stood. I was living in a motel. The few belongings I couldn't wear—tools, mostly—were in a distant cousin's garage, ten miles up the highway.

That afternoon, Lester Smart told me in confidence that his business was growing scarce. It was a trend that had continued for some time now, Smart said, as though people didn't trust the government's assertion that the water would spare the dairy, and the roads necessary to support it. Then he paused, as though unsure he should be telling me these details. He continued: "I lose money. I've never lost money at this. But I stay, Holland. I couldn't think of doing anything else."

I asked, "But how long can you continue to support that? Staying open for the sake of it?"

"Not for the sake of it, Holland, for the sake of the people. And I can sustain it long enough, don't you worry."

I knew immediately that Smart's wasn't the only business so afflicted. Even the towns above the flood line were dying. It bolstered in me the desire to leave. Leave and take Poppy with me. I knew it earlier in the morning, in the sagging bed, but could not say it to her. I feared her reaction. I knew she felt tied to this place, securely moored in its slow current, and that staying was, for her, an act of loyalty to Alex, to his memory. But I wanted her to feel, as I did, kicked loose, adrift.

On the first of July, 1958, they blew the last cofferdam. A crew foreman stood nervously by as the prime minister rose on a temporary stage before a large crowd and a battery of cameras. The Right Honourable John Diefenbaker bent at the waist and, using a prop plunger, co-operated in creating the illusion that he was an expert in explosive demolition. A quarter of a mile away, two engineers, crouched next to a dump truck with a radio link to the foreman back on the stage, used real plungers to set off a series of charges that weakened the seemingly haphazard pile of rubble which held the river at bay.

A confused sound rose from the crowds assembled on both sides of the river, well back from the edge behind lines representing the shoreline of the seaway being born before our eyes. It was a mix of cheers and sobbing, of thrill and disbelief.

For months the date had been fixed in our minds. Everything on hold, everything waiting. Now it came, amid the hum of idling machinery, maybe the far-off rumble of rising water, and even the birds seemed nervous, darting, as before a storm. The crickets stopped their droning.

Downriver, where they had cleared away whole towns—the trees and spires and telephone poles, as well as the houses, schools, barns, shops—sat old foundations, like floor plans drawn in stone, silently awaiting the water.

I stood very still. In my heart mingled elation and fear. Poppy was at my side, twisting her feet in the dry earth, and Evey was leaning into her mother's leg. We made our way through the murmuring crowd back to my Dodge and drove to the Sturges house.

We were silent for a long while, sitting again in the kitchen while Evey played quietly. Something in me was ratcheted up, some tension, a fear that the water would soon overtake us. I felt it on my skin. I was bothered, you might say.

"I don't see a single damn reason to stay, Poppy," I finally said. It was the latest instalment in a conversation we'd been having for weeks, one that tended to start up again at dispersed intervals and, since it had no clean solution, end quickly.

"I can't go," she said. "I can't take Evey away from here. It's all I know."

"You can know more."

"Please, Holland. So you get this uncle to get you a job and you're set up. Wonderful. What do I do in Toronto? The name alone scares me. What kind of a life does Evey get?"

"Something new. There's nothing new here."

"Be fair, Holland. I can stay at Smart's and you can open a garage. There's chances."

"And we can watch all those chances float by us, day after day. Before long we'll die here, Poppy, and nothing will have changed."

"And that's the worst thing in the world, is it? Maybe having you in my life is all the change I needed."

That night the temperature dropped, as though the still-rising waters brought with them a new climate. I woke early and crept downstairs, the hair standing on my neck. I opened the window above the kitchen sink. Half-eaten crab apples, chaff scattered in the wind. I stood at the sink, filling the coffee kettle. It was an unarticulated belief of mine that the nature of a given day was determined in large measure by the quality of the first sip of coffee. On this cool Wednesday, I made a large pot so there would be some left for her. Upstairs, she and Evey slept on.

That afternoon, from a pay phone off the highway, I called my uncle.

Inundation took three days. Three days to wash away better than a hundred years of enterprise.

At the end of those three days, there was an enormous lake, and a new waterway. In the new towns the sawdust still hung in the air. It was no biblical deluge, no great, sudden wave, but a slow and deliberate editing of landscape. You could check it in the morning and go away for a while, and when you looked again you might not be certain the water had risen, until you began to remember the things you had seen before that you could not see any longer. Gradually it rose, ineluctable and ordained—a flood decreed by legislation, enacted by determination.

On the third day, I left.

There is nothing to call it but cowardice. Cowardice and panic. I let those things guide me west, to Toronto.

I started in the McCowan Yard in mid-August, maintaining streetcars, the big shed there like the inside of a blast furnace. By the time the leaves turned, my life felt like a separate existence, completely turned over, not much connected at all to the one I had left in Loucksville.

I was distracted, at least, in Toronto. I repaired streetcars. I lived alone. I ate alone. The exigencies of constructing this new life for myself didn't allow much time to reflect on the question of happy or not happy.

My time with Poppy was an unresolved note. I expected she was hoping I'd return, and I hoped she would join me in the city, simply ring my bell one day. But neither of us capitulated. I came to believe that it had been too great a time—two months which had felt like two years—and it no longer seemed possible to contact her at all. That's how it is when life is complicated by too many details.

I did not see, right away, how my life would feel in the days afterwards. Laid out like a plain, spreading. A delta.

I came to it only later, gradually.

I was in a bachelor apartment on Bloor Street, preparing coffee. The water from the faucet was cloudy. My mechanic's coveralls hung on a hook by the door. The streets were still quiet, the light soft. The grounds were stale.

And I saw that I had lost everything.

That every last thing of value had ebbed from my life, been swept clean away. Gone in the hard way of losing, as of things washed down in a flood.

But so, too, had ten thousand other people watched the land they knew get covered over. And now they watched international shipping glide overtop their old lives. Towns were gone, new ones had been built. Cemeteries were either moved or lost. Businesses relocated or simply ceased to exist.

In the downriver run of a life, rushing from the source to the great, limitless whole, there are innumerable turns, changes in course. A decision, or a missed opportunity. For the most part they are inexplicable. They simply are.

The new waterway had given me a new life—one I hadn't wanted. But it was the one I had. And though I was well installed within it, it did not prevent me from picturing how things might have otherwise been.

I could imagine myself still in Loucksville.

I could see Poppy there, and Evey.

The three of us in the kitchen of Poppy's house, where from the window above the sink I could just barely see a sliver of the water. Silently, in the bluster of an autumn afternoon, a freighter slipping west, loaded perhaps with ore, on its steady way to Duluth, or to Detroit, there to be made into something new.

THE OUTLET

IT WAS EARLY AFTERNOON when they motored into the Outlet, on an aluminum fourteen-footer they'd put in at the north end of Charleston Lake at seven-thirty that morning. A Friday at the end of June, just ahead of the long weekend. The roads and waterways would soon be choked with celebrants, travellers, families.

Weston Hill was quietly anxious to get the weekend started. But first he had to finish creeling the anglers' hauls. It was an exercise aimed more at training his tagalong for the day, a summer-student hire named Cara Franklin, than at collecting any useful figures. Hill understood this was an opportunity to shepherd a future Natural Resources employee. It would require a bit of talking, and he was better at showing than saying, but he would call up the words as required.

One of the first things he said to her, before she had a chance to take her first sip of coffee, was, "I knew your dad."

"Oh, yeah," Cara said politely. "Lots of people did."

"He was good. A good CO."

"I know he loved it."

"That was clear," said Hill. "It showed. In what he did. The way he did things."

Cara was an only child, born when Bob Franklin and his wife, Geena, were both nearing forty. Bob took retirement at fifty-five, when Cara was busting to get her driver's licence, and he kicked around the house awhile, going fishing more mornings than he didn't and getting home as Cara was leaving for school. Then he had a heart attack one afternoon and died in the ambulance.

Whereas her mother hobbled on like it was a leg she'd lost instead of a husband, Cara spent a year or so in utter despair, thinking there really wasn't any way to recover. Then suddenly, one day, she discovered that there was. She knew, without knowing how she knew, that weathering grief was just something a person did. The fact of it began to pull at her like a gravitational force, bending her trajectory toward biology and conservation, until she realized that what she intended to do was to follow her dad's example and become a conservation officer.

Two years into a biology degree at Queen's, she applied for a summer position with the Kingston area office of the Ministry. On the phone she was slick and confident, and during the interview she was some best version of herself, assertive and quick to display her fresh knowledge. She was hired, of course, though there were other good candidates, many of them from her program. For all this bureaucracy's avowed blindness, knowing someone or being someone's kid was still the best way to find yourself more or less where you wanted to be.

They spent the morning intercepting fishing boats, asking about the anglers' catches, how long they'd been on the water, and in most cases checking the coolers and tanks where the landed fish were kept. The sun charted across a flawless sky. Flies skimmed the water and tried to find their way behind the lenses of Cara's sunglasses.

After a bagged lunch, eaten while they were adrift out on the flat water, Hill expressed a desire for ice cream. Cara, assuming he was speaking in the theoretical, offered what she hoped might be interpreted as a polite giggle, but Hill crumpled up his brown paper bag, downed the last of a warm can of iced tea, and swung his leg across the bench so that he was astride it. Then, in a short and violent motion, he pulled at the cord. The Evinrude outboard choked and sputtered and shook, and then caught, jiggling to life beneath them. He throttled up and they were underway. Which was fine with Cara—ice cream sounded good about now.

"Spot called the Outlet," Hill said. "Little summertime place."

"Great," called Cara.

They skipped across the lake's surface for a few minutes, engine in full whine, until the land began to close in around them. Hill eased off the throttle and they crawled slowly over more shallow water, the treed and rocky shoreline quite near, the occasional building—small shacks and cottages, old boathouses on rotting logs—slumping into the water. After a passage so narrow that wheat-coloured reeds rasped against the boat's aluminum sides, the water opened up a bit.

They entered what seemed like a small harbour, maybe thirty or forty yards across, its shoreline crowded with boathouses. At the far end was a public dock, quite busy. On a boat ramp next to the dock, a mean-looking craft was being backed in on its trailer; several more trailers bearing cruisers and bow riders and bass boats waited in the gravel lot just behind. Past the ramp and dock, a small bridge carried a narrow two-lane road over Wiltse Creek, which snaked its way over from the Gananoque River to meet Charleston Lake. This, Cara surmised, was what gave the outlet its name.

They tied up at the public dock—Cara taking extra care with her clove hitch—and climbed up onto the wooden platform. The dock's planks were new, its edges clean. She nearly tripped when she caught the toe of her boot on the spare oars stowed against the side of the boat, but recovered herself and stood erect, removing her sunglasses, tucking her floppy green cotton ball cap embroidered with the blue-and-green Ontario Parks logo under her arm. She reached up with her right hand and wiped a flat palm across her damp brow.

Hill led her up a short path to the side of the road. They waited for a hydro truck to rumble past, then crossed to the combination convenience store/ice cream counter/café, which sat beside the spot where the creek became the lake. As they mounted the three wooden steps at its entrance, the screen door creaked open and then clapped shut. Two teenage girls in bikinis and aviator sunglasses burst out, cradling cold two-litre bottles of Pepsi. They looked local, Cara thought, watching them cross the road in their bare feet. Something about their ease. One of them wore a camo trucker cap, its brim folded severely into a peak, her ponytail pulled through the semicircular hole in the back. Country girls.

Inside, they waited in line for a family in matching cargo shorts and Toronto Blue Jays tank tops to order soft serve, then bellied up to the glass cabinet to look down at the tubs of ice cream there. Cara went first, at Hill's silent insistence—a nod of his reddened head toward the counter—and asked for one scoop of pralines and cream in a small cone. Then Hill stepped up, ordered vanilla, two scoops.

"On me," he said.

They went out a second screen door onto a deck with a southern exposure that stood over the creek. There were three plastic tables with faded Coke-branded umbrellas, around one of which sat the family they'd just seen inside. Cara sat down at another, closest to the store's blue-stained wooden siding, while Hill stood by the flaking white wooden railing and looked out toward the lake.

She thought he looked more than a little ridiculous. Hill was an enormous, ruddy, thick-legged man in khaki shorts, green rubber boots halfway up his shins, an olive short-sleeved shirt, wraparound angler's sunglasses, and a broad-rimmed hat on his head. Yet he was bent reverentially, deferentially, over a very small ice cream cone, taking small licks from it, a white dot of ice cream visible on his tongue for a quick moment before it disappeared into his mouth. In his large and toughened mitt, it looked like a kiddie cone.

The still, warm, slightly rotting scent of the lake came to Cara then on a small puff of wind. It struck her wrong, expecting as she was to smell the cool sweetness of ice cream.

"Hell's bells," Hill said, and took another lick of his cone.

Cara looked about, as if he was somehow sensitive or perceptive to something that eluded her. She was still at an age where she felt it right, much of the time, to defer to the supposed knowledge and experience of her elders; she hadn't yet learned better.

The truth was, Hill was often uttering quips or non-sequiturs that meant something less than what people might assume. He'd long ago identified deep within himself a nervousness about this inability to register piercing or insightful observations about the world. It was a feeling made worse just now with Cara being as young as she was, and with their professional relationship arranged the way it was, and with her being Bob Franklin's kid, and with Bob Franklin being dead. She would be looking to absorb his wisdom, he felt. A kind of surrogacy.

In general, he found the presence of young people—even his own daughter—moderately unsettling. Such encounters forced him to recover a piece of the person he might once have been. Either he would find the younger person insufferable, or so dazzling as to make plain the difference between his own younger self and the person he had become.

It was not gradual. Aging. It did not occur piecemeal, but rather came all at once. He woke up one morning and suddenly realized that youth was a thing apart. A distant province—or worse, because at least provinces could be accessed. No, youth was a memory.

He was already forty-seven and counting the days, literally the days, until retirement. And here, in Cara, was the very sort of person—one so totally unlike him—who would eventually supplant him. It was negation that he feared, at the bottom of it all.

And his only defence was to make remarks about the weather.

A slow-moving cloud—the only one—scudded the sun and seemed to break Hill's attention. He gobbled the last of his sugar cone, wiped his mouth with a napkin, and wadded it up. Cara, who'd already finished her ice cream, stood and, out of habit, turned to see if she was forgetting anything. Then she followed after Hill down the deck's wide steps and across the road toward the dock.

"She'll be a perfect weekend," he said. "Sunny. Twenty-five, twenty-seven. Made plans?"

Shyly, she answered, "Toronto. To meet some friends."

And, truthfully, to get a little high.

Everything was in disarray. Most days she could deal with that. She could lay herself across the jumbled pile of it all and stretch out, find an equilibrium, a baseline, or at least make it look to the rest of the world like she knew what balance was. Whenever a cashier asked if she wanted her receipt, for example, Cara would always say *yes. Yes, please*. Even though each time, without fail, without even so much as skimming it, she would crumple that receipt and throw it into a garbage at the first opportunity. Because, in accepting the offer, sometimes enthusiastically—*determinedly* was actually the word—she was demonstrating to the world that she had her shit together. As though she was going to add the slip of thermal paper to the appropriate labelled envelope and at month's end engage in some serious accounting. As though she knew what responsibility was. As though she had some idea of how it was executed, how it was performed.

The idea had begun to dawn on her that everybody was doing the same act.

So now she was looking not for a mode of life, but for a model of living. Not a role to inhabit, but a new way to simply traverse one minute to the next. Which meant looking outside her own narrow life and the people who populated it. To insert herself into some new and unfamiliar scenario. To remove the safety girding that surrounded her, though the terror that inspired shook her as much as it thrilled her. She was tired from all the shaking and thrilling.

They could have, for the purpose of their survey, remained at the Outlet, done their allotted hours checking anglers' catches, calculating catch per unit effort and so on, then packed up and called it a day. But there were no boats returning just now, and Hill didn't feel like waiting. He wanted to get back out on the water. The sun was high and brutal, and sitting on the dock would feel worse than if they were skipping across the top of Charleston Lake, generating their own breeze.

They each loosened one of the boat's lines and pushed off. Hill yanked the starter line and, when the motor caught, sat astride the bench. He moved the boat in a wide circle until they were facing the mouth of the inlet, then pushing through it, then beyond it, the land on either side sliding away from them.

Hill figured that, in his rumoured youth, he had been attracted to the same sorts of things Cara was—or, at least, he hadn't been as cowed and confused as they left him now. He, too, had spent weekends in Toronto. One night, he and Bill Frady had closed the Horseshoe Tavern, then forgot where Bill's truck was parked and fell asleep at either end of a bench beneath the CN Tower. A security guard woke them up, told them they had to keep moving. They found the truck by accident shortly before the sun came up, and ate breakfast at a counter in the bus station before hauling their asses out of town and back to their basement apartment in Lindsay, two hours away.

Not long after, Hill moved to Kingston, where he had secured a twelve-month contract with the Ministry. Kingston was where he met Karen. Karen, who either miraculously missed all his glaring faults or was willing to overlook them, he was never sure which. The moment he met her was the moment he'd later believe that his adult life began.

Thereafter, the milestones—marriage, first boat, mortgage, permanent job—piled up in a kind of somnambulant parade, as though the only agency required of him was the willingness to remain present.

Occasionally he did feel a greater degree of control, felt capable of harnessing loose energies in order to disrupt life's routine. Like when he'd surprised Karen with a trip to an all-inclusive in Cuba for their tenth anniversary. But mostly he was content to keep his expectations at eye level. That, he felt, was the secret to preventing the world from letting him down. It was an approach that still left him opportunities for pretty sublime experiences. Misty sunrises over various lakes. That August night he and Karen spent with their sleeping bags zipped together on the shore of Canisbay Lake, the moon so full it was almost vulgar, the stars' proximity startling, like he could reach up and brush them, feel their jagged tips with his fingertips. The multiplicity of smells in her hair over-whelming him. Shampoo and lake water and woodsmoke. The colour and the feel of all that. He could never convey it with language. It was not in him. But he kept the shapeless thought of it in the pocket nearest his heart.

It was on a night not too long after the Cuba trip that Karen told him, over kitchen-table beers, that she thought she might be pregnant. Hill thought he was ill-prepared to be a father, or, at any rate, was certain that just about any-body else would be better equipped for it than he. He didn't like moving into circumstances with uncertain outcomes, and this was the most wildly uncertain set of outcomes with which he'd ever been presented. But Karen figured they ought to embrace it anyway. It was his love for and faith in her that made him agree. At the time, she was working the counter at a tire shop and, after a series of contracts, he'd landed a permanent Fish and Wildlife tech position in the Kingston office. He figured they could afford another mouth, if nothing unexpected popped up.

And then Abigail was born big and healthy and shiny-eyed, and before long, he couldn't remember life before her. Every day was something new, a fresh set of wonders.

When Abigail was ten years old, Hill was stabbed in the right eye with a sewing needle. She'd left it on his pillow one night after using it to replace her Barbie's hair, poking yarn through the holes left after she'd pulled all the original hair out. In the dead of the next morning, when Hill rolled over, the needle went through his eyelid and poked into the white of his eye, but only just. He felt the sharp twinge, felt it more as the muscles of his eyelid contracted, and then he reached up and batted the thing away, heard it land on the cherry laminate floor. His vision seemed fine, but as a matter of course he went to the emergency room on Stuart Street in Kingston, where the doctor marvelled at his luck while confirming the lack of serious injury. "Keep an eye on it," was the doctor's advice, laughing at that before shuffling off to see people with real injuries, severe illnesses, waning hope.

Hill didn't blame Abigail, but he did ask her to be more careful with her things.

Life was a strange parade. And when he thought about such things—uncanny things, amazing, beautiful, puzzling things—he had a habit he could not explain, of whistling a two-note trill. He whistled those notes now, as they navigated the narrow passage, watching the lake bottom drop away from them, down beneath the clear, unexcited water.

The boat needled into the heart of the afternoon.

There was a kind of terror in Cara's heart. She had an unbidden sense of her future lying somewhere just ahead; having set herself on a course to progress directly into it, the opportunity to deviate from it lessened with each passing moment.

Hill, on the other hand, appeared happy. Satisfied.

"How did you get into the MNR?" she shouted to him over the motor, as a way of alleviating her own doubts.

"Rocks," he said, and when she stared at him in confusion, he said, "Geology. Started there. Switched to fish. Don't know why, exactly, except that it seemed more likely I'd find work that way. Or I don't know. Maybe I just came to see that I'd rather work with live things than with dead rock."

"Rocks are interesting."

"Sure. But they just sit there. Unless you're talking about millions of years. That's when you see change." He spoke just below a shout over the Evinrude's nasal roar. "But I didn't feel like waiting around for that."

"You seem to love what you do," she said, as much question as statement.

"It wasn't about love. Never saw it as important, about loving what you do, how important that's supposed to be. But it came to be that way, yeah."

"It means something, though."

"This work? Well. Your dad certainly thought so. Had ideas about that."

Hill was not looking at her, but beyond her, to the water their bow was approaching and overcoming, through his plastic wraparounds. The sound of the outboard rose and fell according to its cycles, a poorly tuned machine whanging away to produce inefficient motion.

"He went straight into it," he finally said. "Head-on. Knew what he meant to do."

Certainty, they both thought to themselves, was desirable.

"My dad said he always knew."

"They still had the CO school in Dorset then. Sign up there, stick it out, and you were set. Couldn't help but wind up with a job."

"Easy," offered Cara.

"No, I don't expect it was. Not that your father wasn't cut out for what he did. He was. He was very good at it."

Despite the compliment paid to her own father, Cara felt rebuked, as if perhaps Hill meant to make her feel out of her depth. "I'm kind of making it up as I go along," she said.

"Yeah, they don't make it easy on you, do they? There's no clear path."

"I called like seven different COs to ask how they got where they are."

"Got seven different answers, I bet."

"At least."

"You'll figure it out. The difference now is what the government's willing to show you in terms of loyalty. No security. You'll be contract or seasonal or temporary."

"I think that's everywhere, though. I think that's just how things are going."

"Yeah, I suppose," he said, and tightened his grip, twisting the throttle open. The motor screamed, and Cara had to brace herself as the nose planed upward. He was apparently done with the subject.

Even in the breeze skimming off the water, she was hot. The backs of her knees were wet. She felt laid out, exposed, broiled. The afternoon hours stretched out before her, thick and slow. She felt scrutinized. How would a person ever know all they needed to know?

Ahead of them, shimmering mirage-like above the lake's glinting top, rested half a dozen boats of black, silver, white, nudged against a shallow sandbar. Hill eased back on the throttle as they neared, and as the boat came to a halt with one final lurch, Cara heard the sand abrasive against their hull. Hill wrenched out a spring-loaded pin on the motor's housing and tilted the whole thing up so that the screw was out of the water. Then he replaced the pin in a second hole, and the motor stayed where he'd raised it.

"Afternoon, guys," Hill said to the anglers, and they were all guys. Of course they were.

Cara remained silent behind him as he took the bow rope in his hand and leapt out onto the wet sand.

"Just wanted to survey your catches, if we could."

"You Conservation?" asked one man with a comically large, drooping moustache. He sat in a new-looking bass boat, a gleaming showroom piece with built-in depth finder and a nifty little silent electric motor to move about, once he'd cast, without alarming the aquatic life.

It probably cost as much as a house, Cara thought.

"This is just research, guys," Hill said, "not enforcement. Nobody's getting a ticket."

Cara felt an urge to attach herself to his authority, then just as suddenly felt a revulsion at the idea, and was seized by a need to differentiate herself, to claim some distance. She wondered if she could accomplish this with a facial expression directed at the fishermen, but couldn't decide on which expression, so she settled for holding her mask rigid beneath her ball cap and aviators.

Hill took notes as the men offered the details of their catches. After a few minutes, he turned to Cara, who'd been standing in their boat watching, and said, "You should get some experience filling these out." So she too stepped out onto the sand and watched, over his shoulder, as he recorded with a stubby pencil on waterproof forms. Mostly they'd caught bass, both largemouth and small, as well as perch, lake trout, and some rock bass. One boatload of Americans had a pile of pumpkinseed. It was so rote, he could have guessed at it all and been about ninety percent on the money. Hill handed the hinged stainless steel folder to Cara—an uptick in her level of responsibility—so she could fill out more details, recording lengths and rough weights, as well as how long the anglers had been at it.

Most of them had been on the water since before day-break, but a couple had just shown up. Recreational fisher-men, her dad would have said. Just out for the sunshine and a chance to get away from the day-to-day. Nothing wrong with that.

After they'd spent forty minutes on the sandbar, they bid the anglers good afternoon, climbed back in the boat, and pushed off, drifting slowly backwards until the water was deep enough. Hill pulled the pin, dropped the outboard back into the water, and pull-started it to life.

"One more spot," he shouted over the whine. "Public ramp. That'll be enough for today. Then we can take it in, get this tub out of the water, and head home."

Cara nodded. "Sounds good," she said.

Hill had a moment of anger then, built up from frustra-tion at the way the day was unfolding. Impatience.

He had wanted Cara to be more assertive. That was part of it. He'd admired her father, saw in him a roll-up-your-sleeves ethos to which he related deeply—a getting-things-done spirit that resided more behind the breastbone than it did behind the eyes—and he wanted her to show him something that reminded him of her father. A bit of spit in the eye. But he wasn't seeing that from Cara.

Hill whisper-whistled his two-note refrain. He told himself that she'd come to it eventually, once she got out of school and was forced to really encounter the world, had cut her legs in the shaggy thatch of things as they were.

He was reminded, again, of his old Lindsay roommate, Bill Frady, now an area biologist in Peterborough. Frady had done his graduate work with wolves in Killarney, spent a season tranquilizing and tagging them. And the amazing thing was, after that, no dog trusted him. Even though he'd always been a dog person. Was going to get one to take fowl hunting with him and so forth. But they'd growl when he entered the room, snap if he got close. Hill had seen this on several occasions, over many years now. It was the damnedest thing. There was some kind of a stink that Frady couldn't shake, and dogs couldn't help but notice.

It was life's great lesson: you can't get away from yourself, not for long. Your head can float, get you lost behind your own eyes until you think you're somewhere else, that you're someone else, but sooner or later, and often thereafter, there'd come something sudden and real to bring you right back to concretenesses.

Cara was looking ahead to her weekend, which promised a man named Trevor and a borrowed apartment in Leslieville. Cheap beer, Korean fried chicken, loud rooms, cryptic Facebook status updates, sex on a rooftop, 3 AM shawarma, sleeping late, brunch. Trevor was not someone she saw when she looked very far into her future, but he featured prominently in the next seventy-two hours, and she was happy about that.

But something in Hill's carriage, his know-it-all practicality, suggested that her excitement was somehow unbefitting an adult—which, as both present parties understood, was the goal here, to look and act and think as an adult. It made her a little angry. If she, goddammit, if she chose to spend a couple of careless days with someone with whom she saw no future, someone who frankly couldn't even hold up his end of a conversation, but knew where to go and how to have fun, whose business was it?

She and Trevor shared a joke.

He'd once asked her why she never looked at him with puppy-dog eyes. "You want some other girl for that," she said. "Best you'll get from me is dead-puppy-dog eyes." And then she rolled her eyes back into her head and stuck out her tongue, holding that for a moment before beginning to laugh. Trevor laughed, too, and it became an inside joke. Dead-puppy-dog eyes. Sometimes Trevor would leave the room and when he'd come back Cara would be lying on her back with her arms and legs bent at each joint, her eyes blank, her tongue lolling.

These crude and louche things were dear to her. And if Toronto, that worldly venue, that place of choice and noise, that dense concrete maze, dazzled and excited her, why not go there? Did going there exclude this place, the lake's spray in her face, the hot sun, the green shores?

It seemed to her that it did not.

It seemed to her that it was possible to love both.

But Cara wasn't terrifically interested in explaining that to Weston Hill just now. To open her mouth was to open herself to ridicule for her choices. So she kept quiet.

Hill apparently felt no such compunction, however. As the Evinrude settled back into its high, constant sound and the bow cleaved the lake to either side of them, he said through his sunglasses, "You know what I think about sometimes is how your dad was in '96."

"The strike?"

Hill nodded. "He was so committed. Stood in front of cars, banged on hoods. Got into managers' faces. There were people who never spoke to him again."

"I never heard about any of that."

"You were a baby, I think."

"Sure, but even later. Nothing about all that."

"You were just a kid, a little kid, and you were gonna be protected from all that. When they ended it, five weeks in, there was a party at Ray Wynne's house. People getting blackout drunk. I mean, just a total mess. Really. Puking, pissing drunk."

She was certain he'd included this bit just to impinge on her delicate, young-lady sensibilities.

"But your dad has, I think, one beer. Sits in a corner look-ing serious. Because he knew. Whatever money we won wouldn't add up to anything but a loss, you work it out. It was no-win. And the night ends and your father drives everybody home. Loads a bunch of people in the truck, takes them each to wherever they need to go, comes back for another load."

Since she was entertaining the emotion, this angered her, too: how Hill seemed to be claiming her father, as though knowing him as an adult somehow gave Hill something she could never have.

Fuck you, she thought. *He changed my diaper and taught me to fish and he barbecued my hamburgers until they were like hockey pucks.*

Cara sat right up front with each of her hands braced against the gunwales, her arms stiff, her palms flat on the hot metal. The sun beat overhead, but behind them—beyond Hill, should Cara turn to look at him—the clean blue horizon had suddenly tinted violet. The wind, hot, began to jab and gust.

In the newly roiled air, Hill seemed to make a decision. "Weather's coming," he said. "Let's call it a day."

"Sure?"

He cut north then, abruptly, jostling Cara where she sat on the hard aluminum bench. "Hold on," he called too late, and opened up the motor to move with great speed across the middle of the lake, back toward the marina where their day had begun.

When they pulled close to the public dock, he cut the motor, and she—momentarily wanting to feel capable—stood and held a foot out in space, waiting to step up onto the broad planks and catch the boat. She did so, then walked the boat up toward shore and tied it off. Hill tossed her the keys to the truck. He began offloading their things onto the dock as Cara nervously backed the trailer down the ramp and parked it, the lake lapping over the trailer's wheels and consuming its trusses. Over their hot heads, clouds folded like batter and the air took on a green, aqueous light.

Hill untied the boat and backed it off, then aimed the nose into the centre of the trailer. He gunned it forward, and missed. "All my previous accomplishments account for nothing," he said, "but this my labour shall measure me."

Christ, Cara thought. *Another martyr.*

She waded down into the water and attempted to catch the boat by its gunwales, but before she could, a frustrated Hill cut the motor and jumped into the water himself. Hands clamped around the aluminum edge, he hauled the boat toward the shore so it would catch in the trailer's little rubber wheels.

While he was thus engaged, his back turned, she realized could reach into the boat, retrieve one of the oars, and swing its broad side into his temple. Lay him out cold. Maybe even kill him, if she chose. She smiled, and then she rolled her eyes back into her head and stuck her tongue out. Dead-puppy-dog eyes.

Then they were in the truck.

Each was experiencing their own impatience, interested primarily in nursing their own private animus, in finding their own paths to the dark end of the day, to their respective ideas of wildness and abandon. Eager for their weekends.

Just get on with it.

Hill looked up at the clouds and whistled. He pulled the white pickup forward, dragging the boat out of the water, dripping, and pointed the nose toward Kingston. They drove most of the way in silence.

No rain ever came, only the threat of it. It would be days before they were hit with a real good storm.

EMMYLOU

SECONDARY HIGHWAYS latticed bankrupt counties, shuttered berry farms, and cedar trees. Weeds consumed empty gas pumps.

Out here, Wendell's Korean subcompact felt inadequate. Perfect for parallel parking, but nothing here required such concision. Out here you could afford to be imprecise. You could park in the tall grass if you wanted and nobody would say boo. You could leave it in a field, and in time it would be accepted as part of the landscape.

I'd been offered respect, kindness, loyalty, and warmth—a home—but grew suspicious and selfish, and fled, which is far from noble, I know, but Wendell had fathered a child somewhere and then bolted. We're from that kind of stock. My dad collected convertibles, DUIs, debt, but was very clear that I'd be solely responsible for bailing myself out of any scrapes. Wendell's father, my uncle Sandy, felt intellectually overmatched in any argument and usually answered with his knuckles.

Cowardice, like the lakeside cabin where we were headed, was something to which my entire family had year-round access.

We turned off the highway and onto the gravelled and signless fire route. The car crept along for ten minutes, then came to a stop beneath big, precarious oaks. We looked upon the cabin, decrepit and listing. The key was on a nail on the underside of the back deck, where it had overwintered for the sixtieth year among the spiderwebs and mouse shit.

Loveless, motherless, we were submerged beneath cartoonish desires to be the men we thought we could be when we were nineteen and twenty-two. But at thirty and thirty-three, we still weren't. It likely had never been possible. That'd been someone's joke.

In the cabin, Wendell stoked a fire in the stove. I put a cassette into the old tape deck, because that's all we had up there. Emmylou Harris sang a Louvin Brothers chestnut and Wendell stared into the flames. We ate stale peanuts and drank coffee mugs full of whisky.

"I just wish I'd had a chance to fall in love with Emmylou Harris," Wendell said, listening.

"She's a Yankees fan," I answered.

"So?"

"So, not perfect."

"I'd get Derek Jeter's face tattooed on my back to have her love me."

"You don't know. Maybe she's awful."

"Listen to her."

He was right.

But what if it was all performance, a stage persona? That's nothing to love, I thought. That's all I've ever given out, and it brings nothing back. I've shortchanged everyone I've ever kissed. But I didn't tell him that.

"She sounds like the most incredible woman in the world," I said, and meant it.

At midnight, we floated in inky water with stars winking overhead and ribbon-like vegetation winding around our bicycling limbs. The water was warm and the air above was cool and clean, and our toes and asses wiggled free and uncovered, while our cocks dangled like unsheathed hunting knives. The mosquitoes buzzed a beautiful drone. *Summer*, we called it, but really that was just a name we'd tacked onto the strange place we'd come to, a place where I'd just sabotaged the best love I was likely to know, while Wendell had chosen weed and sleeping late over a life actually worth pursuing.

It was the middle of June and smelled like it. We swam out through the shallow bay and beyond the mouth of it, to the open water, which was colder, and deep, and as dark as sleep. I wanted to find somewhere to float on my back and mimic my own death, my ears submerged, cradled by water, the darkness all around me. Wendell wanted to go to the little island we'd always called the swimming place and jump in the water from its high stones while shouting Tupac lyrics.

There was a cottage around the bend from the swimming place. I never knew who owned it. It was rented out to city people, so every time we'd go up, there'd be a different group staying, barbecuing their burgers, playing their music, shouting at their children. Wendell swam past the swimming place and toward that cottage, its glass face blank.

Down on the rocks near the shore, there glowed a fire. When I lay still in the water, I could hear women there, their laughter spreading out over the water's surface concentrically, moving over my fevered head.

Wendell hauled himself out onto a rock, a hundred yards away from them, so he could vomit. He hacked and sputtered, then washed his face with lake water and motioned at me to come with him. I slid myself out as soundlessly as possible and stood in the buzzing air next to him. Bare as infants, we walked over the rocks and between the pines and bushes until Wendell stopped behind a tree and leaned over to look at the women.

There were seven of them, in their thirties, I guessed, bright and animated, wine-happy. The fire's orange light carved their faces into caricatures. Wendell stood totally still, but in my peripheral I could see him breathing deeply. There was a watery, animal scent coming off him. I could feel the heat of his haunches, leaning as we were around the other side of the same pine tree, staring. We didn't want to alarm them. I was at once glad and sorry that I wasn't more drunk.

"I wanted to care more than I did," said one of the women, willowy, angular. The others laughed. "But in the end, you know."

It was dead easy to sense their vulnerability. We watched them and they had no idea we were there. I defy you not to feel the awful power in such a scenario. It felt like there was heat in our blood, a physical tell of our grotesque wills. The violence we possessed, though if pressed we'd deny it, always. Even at our lowest, it felt so good to be us, and so terrible. We were gifted with everything anyone could ask for, and we asked for more. We were all cock and skin and teeth. They did not know just how afraid they ought to have been. Even accidentally, we could be brutal. Maybe especially accidentally.

The shortest one noticed us first. She stared furiously at the tree behind which we sheltered, and when something resolved itself out of the darkness—Wendell's face?—she started and said, "Who's there?"

Some of the others gasped in alarm, and they rose as one. One of them held up the stick she'd been using to poke the fire, brandishing it against us, against the shadows.

We turned and hotfooted it down to the water's edge, then threw ourselves in, keeping our heads low. I took great gulping breaths and tried to keep my face underwater as long as I possibly could, crawling forward in that perfect, swallowing darkness. We swam. Our line was direct.

If we'd stuck around and spoken to them, I'd have told them that we posed no threat. All the if onlys. I had a life built out of them.

We hauled ourselves onto the land in the lee of the cabin. Once inside, we towelled off with the terry-cloth rags I'd known since childhood, and drank some more to steady our digits, to thin and cool our blood. Then we slept on a pair of decades-old chesterfields, our jeans rolled up and placed beneath our heads for pillows.

In the morning, we woke coffeeless and ate last year's Raisin Bran for breakfast, dry. We were aware of our own piteousness. Against a cold sky that proffered no clemency, the stove burped a syrupy heat that stretched out minutes and bred in us a disinclination to move.

"Jesus, we're awful specimens," I said to Wendell.

Even absent indictments, there'd been crimes.

Sometime in the night I had dreamed that the willowy one had followed us and, upon finding us, smirked a large, victorious smile, as she'd confirmed for herself all that she'd suspected. We protested, claimed to be victims of our public educations, of our grandmothers' attitudes, of things deep within the structures and biases that supported us. Hazards we could not swerve. Of course, we wished to be innocent, which is distinct from blameless. We wished it so fervently that we believed we were. We felt as though Emmylou had let us down. Emmylou had been our defence—inadequate, silly, convenient, heartfelt.

Wendell and I sipped from mugs of warm water. His: Swedish country aesthetic; mine: *Big Hug Mug*, browned, burnt sienna lettering. We inventoried all we felt was wrong with our lives, produced a list of complaints so mundane it bored us to name them. We talked about what had happened the night before.

"I think they knew it was in good fun," Wendell said.

"I don't believe that you believe that," I said.

"We could be good men," he said.

We had a pretty good laugh about that.

WATERFALLS

ABOUT MY BROTHER'S DEATH there is really very little to say, except maybe that he'd long wanted to die and had finally succeeded in doing so.

Pedro. That wasn't his name, but I'd called him that from a very early age. I don't even know why. His name was Philip. There's no explaining childhood. There's no explaining brotherhood.

Pedro was born two years earlier than I, but he was fifty years wiser. I don't know how these things happen. Before he was shaving, he had plumbed the mysteries of the heart. He told me about all of it from the top bunk, and his voice floated down to me as I lay in my lower berth, staring up at photos of *Star Wars* action figures I'd torn from the *Sears Wish Book* and stapled to the underside of his bunk.

My memories of boyhood are fragments. Pedro and I hucking rocks at a fat light-bulb moon. Where were we? The silver fog coming down upon the fields, fuzzed at its edges by the moon's glare, its coolness slapping our bare baby cheeks. Clouds like dollops of cream in a sky the colour of hot wind, our father baiting our hooks before we dropped them into the amber water of a nameless lake. We had a drinker for an uncle who taught us to curse. Ours was a sunburned and largely happy young life.

It must've been two years ago, at our cousin Barb's wedding. The last wedding I'd attended was my own, to Jane, but Jane had opted out of attending this one.

Pedro and I were finishing the bottles left behind the bar in the large white tent. It was four in the morning. Everything was kind of blurred and blue and sickly-tasting, but we persisted because we thought it was the right thing to do. Barb was our favourite cousin and she was marrying a terrible man, so our protest—our act of mourning for her happiness—was to finish all the liquor and then smash all the bottles on the stage where the cover band had done awful things to the Rolling Stones and the Bay City Rollers.

Pedro held a very large Cuban cigar in his hand, and only occasionally puffed on it. We were wearing crisp and lovely suits we'd bought in a strip mall. Since it was a wedding, we thought ostentatious display was in order.

He wanted to describe for me a trip to Niagara Falls. He told me this:

Pedro and his wife, Rebecca, had reserved a room billed as having a view of Niagara Falls, but when they got there they found that another hotel was blocking their view. All they could see was the river as it neared the lip and the mist that rose above it all. Pedro had wanted to complain, but Rebecca convinced him not to. She said, *It's lovely anyway.* She said, *If you're more interested in looking at a waterfall than you are in looking at me, then we have problems.* He saw her line of reasoning and, though he was stingy with the details, told me they made love with the curtains open and the illuminated mist hanging in the air outside. Then they went to sleep.

She woke, did Rebecca, screaming and panting and staring right through him, whispering about a terrible dream she'd had. Pedro said they should go for a walk to see the falls, so they dressed and headed out into the cool night. At the railing, looking down into that watery hole, Rebecca was glassy-eyed. Pedro said she looked like she was in shock. Not about the falls, though she'd never seen them before, but about whatever it was she'd dreamed.

A man, she said.

They sat on a bench, damp in the mist, and she relayed to him something she'd never told before, a horrible thing that had happened to her in her past, a man who'd hurt her. There were no details to speak of. You know the awful things men can do. Just saying that something had happened brought the tears out of her and inspired in him a murderous rage.

Everything changed, Pedro told me. He said it was like he didn't know her.

My foolish brother, who could not accept that life had occurred before him. I loved him, the idiot, and I threw rocks with him and fished with him and drank with him, and I would do all of these things gladly still, if it were possible. I'd do it all until I die. But Pedro's moral blind spots were sizable. Though filial attachment dictated that I love him, and self-imposed tragedy compels me to hold his memory dear, I would very much like, were he still alive, to slap him with a sock full of nickels.

I wish I'd had the nerve to do it when he first told me, in that mellow post-nuptial tent, spiffed up in our dark suits. But I didn't. I was too full of Lamb's and Malbec and schnapps. I was mellowed, too, by the understanding that his reaction was natural and animal. It's what might occur to any of us. Though maybe some of our most natural inclinations could stand to be smacked out of us.

He told me what he did next: He consoled her. He took her head in his hands and said, *Shh, babe, shh.* He walked her back to the hotel and he gave her one of his Clonazepams and a little tiny bottle of vodka from the mini-bar, and she found sleep right there, on the starchy hotel pillow she'd left an hour earlier. Then he lay in the dark for a good long while, still in his clothes, before finally rising. He slipped out the door and strode once more, agitated, to the falls. At the edge he gripped the railing and fixed his eyes on the line right where those millions of gallons of water tipped over. He ground his teeth together and felt his temples throb. He wallowed in homicidal anger. He yelled. He sobbed. He asked all the gods he didn't believe in why she hadn't told him about this horrible thing when they'd met, or before they'd married, or soon thereafter. Why she'd waited so long. He made it about himself—and that might have been just as damnable as what the other man did to her. Then Pedro took the ring from his finger and he wound up and hurled it like a stone into the tumbling water, where it was lost forever.

He ended his story there, because I knew the rest. They drove back to Toronto in silence. Rebecca moved out. The few times I saw her after they split, I hadn't known why she'd looked so hollowed out; his confession filled in the blanks. She'd put her trust in the man she loved and he turned away. He blamed her. He'd peeled back his ribs and shown her the muck and sewage he kept there. There's no unseeing such a thing.

Our dad, who had himself kept many grudges—against co-workers, bosses, political parties, sports franchises— once said to us, *Grudges are just loyalty to your own animosities*. But there was nothing commendable about what Pedro had done. To feel something does not mean that you need act upon that feeling. You must ask questions of it. You must interrogate it. And after that, even then, it's necessary to leave some things unexpressed.

He came to see that, soon after everything settled down, but by then it was too late. He'd already gone over the edge. Said and done things. There was a blankness in his eyes after that, an obvious regret, knowing what he'd done to her, how he'd compromised the safety of her passage through life.

That, I expect, is why my brother killed himself. Truthfully, he'd always been romanced by death; realizing that he held within himself such cruelty was the best excuse he was ever likely to come across. You can't carry around a thing like that. So he stopped carrying it. Not that it made Rebecca's load any more manageable.

In his note, he left me a canoe. So Jane and I strapped it to the roof of a car and drove up the Bruce Peninsula.

There had been nothing all that noteworthy about the canoe. We were not accomplished canoeists, he and I. We were just two boys, and then two young men, who liked putting ourselves in desperate situations and then fighting our way out of them. That we had done just that on two or three occasions in the canoe was, I think, why he left it to me, and nothing else. I'd have gladly taken his guitar, but that went to someone else.

Still, we thought it was nice of him to pass along a canoe, felt that way even after my half-assed job tying the thing to the roof of Jane's car resulted in it being caught in the stiff wind, sent airborne and then cartwheeling end over end into a ditch somewhere in Bruce County.

We stopped and backed up to look at it, but it was done. Cracked and crushed and useless, the fibreglass splintered and frayed. So we left the damn thing there, and instead of continuing up the peninsula to camp, we turned around and got a motel room in Owen Sound. That's the kind of thing we used to do.

Jane was originally from Oakville and could not be made to forget it. She was Canadian in the way the queen is Canadian: she'd seen only some of it, but felt comfortable ruling it all. I had married Jane in a typical early-twenties fit of confusion and yearning, made her beauty emblematic of the photo-worthy life I wanted to live, to have recorded. I wanted to be envied. I wanted her flawless legs to be the thing people most remembered about me. Her money didn't hurt, of course. I wanted to be comfortable. She loved buying me bottles of good stuff. All I could really give her in return were my looks, and I could see a time when that would no longer cut it. I worried about my hair thinning.

We got along well for a few years at first, but eventually our interactions came to be underlaid with caustic fear. Fear that we'd lashed ourselves to the mast of a doomed clipper, as well as an anger that suggested we blamed each other for the gaping hole in the hull. It made it damned hard to relax, though we found temporary solutions. Mostly they were pharmaceutical.

"This is terrible," Jane said in the motel. "Everything is terrible."

"Am I terrible?" I said.

"Of course you are."

We bought a big bottle of vodka and then we didn't get out of bed for two days. That's how we would remember Owen Sound. We'd say, *Yes, we've been to Owen Sound. Very lovely*.

Later, I wondered what those two days might have been like had we not destroyed my dead brother's canoe.

We'd been kayaking before the somersaulting canoe experience. Someone had told Jane that kayaks were great, so we got a pair, and we tried them, and they were great.

Then someone else told her we should take them to Western Quebec, not far from Ottawa. A chain of lakes there,
she was told. You could go from one to the next to the next,
and it was beautiful, and at night you could stay in these
lovely lakeside inns. So off we went to Western Quebec.

The first lake was beautiful. It was a greyish, windy morning in early July, but the trees and the quiet and the green
water astonished me. Jane paddled next to me. Her kayak
was bright yellow, mine was red. Slow down and stop, they
suggested. We ought to have followed that advice. Instead
we tore ahead in our red life jackets. Everything we needed
was rolled up, zippered, pouched, strapped down. Our
weed was double-bagged, as were all our pills. I had a bottle
of gin between my thighs.

God, it was beautiful.

"Call Toronto," Jane said. "Tell them we're moving. Tell
them we'll never be back. When they ask where we've gone,
tell them the name of this lake, whatever it is."

"Maybe the next one will be even more beautiful," I said.

"What would it cost?" Jane said.

"What would what cost?"

"A lake."

The lakes all had names, but we didn't know them, didn't
care to learn. We stopped between two of them that first
night and an Anglo couple put us up in their little bed and
breakfast.

"I hope we meet nothing but Anglos," Jane said. She was
wearing only underwear and a sports bra and was splayed
out atop the checkered bedspread, waiting for her pills to
kick in.

"It might be nice to talk to some real Québécois people,"
I said.

"You and the French," she said. She looked at her phone, which had been tucked into a waterproof pouch between her legs all day. "Everything is lame. Awful and lame. Facebook is worst of all."

"I keep up with my mother on Facebook," I said.

"I hate your mother," she said.

"I think everybody knows that, Janey."

The television in our room didn't work, and the owners neglected to mention that the tap water would smell the way it did. We sucked on the bottle of gin and slept deeply.

In the morning, after a large breakfast, we resumed our trip. That day's lake was emerald and amber, truly one of the most beautiful places I'd ever seen. Hills rose on all sides, heavily treed and interrupted only here and there by the clean lines of tasteful homes. There was absolutely no wind, so we glided like ball bearings across a flawless surface. Painted turtles sunned themselves on logs. When we got near, they plopped into the water with the suddenness of stones.

The middle of the lake was not terrifically deep. As we floated there, I could see right down through the green water to the dark and weedy bottom.

"There," Jane said. She was pointing off toward the farthest shore, to the west, to a blot of white amid all the green. It was a little waterfall, crashing over the grey solidity of rocks.

Her beauty was so cruel. It stung me, needing it so badly.

"Imagine the fur traders coming to this," I said. "They'd have portaged it. Right there. I bet you anything that's the portage route." There was a little trail next to the water which disappeared into the woods, it was true, but I was just talking. I didn't know anything.

"There were no fur traders here," Jane said.

"Like hell! Look at it. Imagine all the foxes and raccoons and beavers. I bet somebody told King Louis about it personally. This is *coureur des bois* territory, Janey!" I was a little drunk on the desire to be smarter than she was.

"*Coureur des bois?*"

"Look it up."

"One semester in Montreal doesn't make you an expert on francophone culture. Neither does fucking a couple of them."

There had been four. Five.

We paddled toward the waterfall. It was the end of a short river, an outlet where the next lake up the chain came spilling into this one. Maybe thirty feet wide and ten or twelve feet tall, the waterfall churned down over and between solid hunks of granite. Before the point where it began falling, the water was a deep, cool green; after, it was foamy and white. As we paddled nearer, we felt the coolness and the push of the current produced by the fall. There was a mineral taste at the back of our throats, an airiness we felt in our eyes. A mist settled on the skin of our faces and forearms.

The elemental violence of the thing was not unsexual. Something about the churn and force of it all made me want to disrobe and let it pummel me flat. I wanted to be on the wrong end of catastrophe just so I could hear that rushing water sound filling my ears. I wanted to be pulled apart in a riot of green and white bubbles. Sometimes you consider trading it all in for a moment of exhilaration, and you know in your heart of hearts it'd be worth it. But you hold off because there are people who love you and they'd be upset, or because there's a movie you haven't seen yet.

Jane must have been thinking the same sensual thoughts. She pointed her paddle at the shore and some rocks and trees there, and I got her meaning. We pulled up and hobbled out of our crafts, tied them to a pair of cedar trees. The waterfall roared next to us. We were on somebody's land, some cottager or wealthy retiree, but that meant nothing to us. Me and Jane, we don't tend to respect property rights unless it's our own property in question. We're like most people that way.

All of a sudden, Jane was standing there on a boulder wearing only a bathing suit. It was black and sleek and it made her look like a gorgeous seal, slippery and firm. I doffed my shirt and stood only in my shorts. I was, for a few years, a person who could take his shirt off anywhere.

We leapt into the water together, hand in hand. It was a dishonest gesture; we were taking no plunge. We'd taken it years before, and all it got us was wet.

The water was cool. We whooped and hollered. The current kept pushing us out to the middle of the lake, but we swam into it and found purchase on rocks on either side of the falls. There we could stick our fingers into little crags and cracks and then let go and have the water push our bodies backwards, like flags in a stiff breeze. The noise made it impossible to hear one another, so a silence was enforced. It was like a form of therapy. It was blissful.

Jane began edging herself forward, toward the heart of the falls, moving hand over hand along the rocks. When she got right up next to them, she turned with her back to the rock and dove off toward the whitest water, the spot where the falls hit the lake. She was lost from sight, pushed down and out. I had a moment of concern, so I stuck my head under the water to see if I could spot her. She was down there, through a curtain of dark green and dancing white, a black-and-white form highlighted by the sunlight slicing down through the water. On or near the bottom she paused, and stayed down there a beat longer than I thought she would, then shot toward the surface, emerging with her mouth in a big O, her eyes wide.

"Waaah!" she cried. "Oh wow, oh wow! It's so beautiful!"

She looked happy and unburdened. It was a rare thing for her.

After we'd swum another few minutes—leaping like dolphins into and out of the spray, arcing our bodies to point down toward the bottom, surfacing like corks, letting the current push us around—we ambled up onto the shore and stood in the clean sun on the rocks, dripping dry. We untied our kayaks and climbed in, pushed off, and floated away.

In the middle of the lake, Jane said to me, "Babe, I've lost my ring," and she showed me her bare finger.

"Holy shit," I said.

"You know how my hands shrink when they're cold. It must have been dragged away by the force of the water," she said.

"Holy shit," I said again.

"Oh, babe," she said. "It's just a thing. It isn't anything more than that. A hunk of metal. It just happened. We can get another."

"Sure," I said.

"Or not. We're not symbol people," she said, though she might have said *simple people*.

"Sure. No."

"You get hung up on the smallest things. Let's keep paddling and then find somewhere to stay tonight, and we'll get drunk and you can debauch yourself all over me. That'll make you feel better."

"Are you happy, Janey?"

"Oh, Jesus," she said. "Not this. I can't. I won't. Just paddle."

We were the only people in the world for each other. It crushed us to know it because love was so awful. All love in general, but ours in particular. Losing her ring was her reaction to that—to being in love with someone she hated.

I knew then what she must have been doing at the bottom of the lake. A moment of clarity under ten feet of uproarious water. She had felt the strong water thumping into her rib cage and musculature, and decided to let her ring drift away.

She never—and we were together three more years after that—she never said anything about all this to me directly, but her act sent a clear message to me. I was amazed she hadn't sent it sooner.

But there'd been love there. I see that now. I know it because if things had been different—if Jane had told to me what Rebecca had told to Pedro—I'd have felt just as affronted and repulsed as he had. We're terrible, really. It isn't the act of loving that's awful, but the people who do the loving. It troubles me to know that I wouldn't have been any better.

EX-FATHER

A LIGHT SNOW was falling. The flakes looked like packing material, tumbling so slowly and evenly they appeared as a cloud of suspended particulate that the earth and all its accessories were being lifted slowly through. It was a Sunday afternoon in April, and quiet. A rare still point in Sarah Lee's hectic life, a few hours of slow time with her boy, Ry. They played tic-tac-toe with crayons on a big scroll of paper and then ate cookies while watching TV, the crumbs falling to their chests and on the blanket they shared.

Then Sarah Lee's ex-father, Reg—and she called him Reg, because she didn't want to honour him with Dad—came limping up the front step and rang the bell.

Sarah Lee opened the door and saw him there, the snow coating his shoulders and bare head, a battered vinyl suitcase in one hand.

"Jesus," she said.

"Surprise," he said. Then he sang, atonally, *"Nobody doesn't like Sarah Lee."*

"Ha ha," she said, but it hadn't been funny to her as a kid and it wasn't funny now. She was trying to decide if he'd shown up to prove to her that he was now harmless, or that he still presented a threat to her and to all the people in his life. He looked pretty beaten down. She let him in her door, but she did not hug him. "What do you want here? Last I knew, you were a security guard in Memphis."

"Knee's in ruins," he said, bending and holding the left one up slightly. "Came back home to get it repaired."

"Okay."

"Recovery's six months. Minimum."

"You're kidding me."

She looked out at the falling snow, and then at his shoes, which were worn and flapping and clearly soaked through, and she knew she was stuck with him. As awful as what he'd done to her and her mother was, she still felt obliged, as his only acknowledged child, to help. She wished she didn't, but there was no way out from behind it.

"Well, come in, I guess," she said, then took his bag and set it down next to a recycling bin while he took off his shoes and unbuttoned his coat. "My boy's just in here watching the TV." She led him into the warm, dim room where Ry was still wrapped up in a blanket on the couch. The TV shouted.

"What's his name again," Reg asked, as though he had ever remembered.

"Ry."

"Ry. Hey, Ry. Hello there."

Ry was in first grade, and not adjusting particularly well. His reading was lagging, he didn't talk about friends, and there were still days he came home having peed himself. He looked away from the screen and stared impassively at the broken bit of a man standing next to his mother.

"I'm your granddad."

The boy looked at his mother, not knowing what to do with that information, and she offered a small nod atop a shrug. That was about the extent of the interaction between the boy and his grandfather. Ry turned his face back to the TV, and Reg went back to displaying as little interest in children as he had when Sarah Lee was a girl.

She led Reg into the kitchen, where he sat at the little round table.

"Get you anything?"

"Drink'd be good."

"Like water? Might have some Diet Coke."

"I'd take a glass of water as a chaser."

"Right. Don't know what I've got," she said. She pulled a chair from the three around the table, moved it over toward the fridge, then stood on it and opened the cabinet overtop. Only in that moment did she realize she'd learned to keep her liquor there from Reg, when she was about five years old.

"I don't have much hard stuff, but I think Tal might've left something."

"That the boy's father?"

"Was, yeah." She pulled down a bottle of Teacher's. "This okay?"

"Sure. More of a breakfast Scotch, really," he said, "but it'll do."

He unscrewed the lid and poured a generous slug of it into a juice glass she put in front of him. Later, she noted, he slipped the bottle into the pocket of his coat and she never saw it again.

The temperature shot upward overnight. By morning the snow was gone and spring appeared to have a decent foothold. Sarah Lee cleaned two houses and was home by the early afternoon.

Soon after, Reg got up off the daybed where she'd put him in the little sunroom off the back of the house. His hours were all off. He either slept dawn to noon, or went from drunk and nasty to hungover and cranky without ever going to sleep. He didn't seem all that different from what her mother had described, except now he hobbled and likely had to go to the bathroom more often than he used to.

They sat on the porch of her rented house, smoking cigarettes, watching a car or two roll by on the road. On a clear day she could see America from where she was sitting, but just barely.

He looked at her through the smoke. "You still have blond hair."

"I know."

"Your mother gave it to you, you know. She went dark right after she had you." His own hair was gone, but it had been sandy brown once.

"I know. She told me that a hundred times, Reg." She added, "It was pink about six months ago," but then chastised herself, because what business was it of his? That or anything else?

A line of pine cones stood atop the porch's railing. Reg flicked his spent butt at them, trying to knock one down into the dwarf spirea on the other side.

"Hey, quit that," Sarah Lee said. "Those are Ry's. Calls them his trees." She stubbed her cigarette out in the lid of a Snapple bottle. "Gotta go get him and bring him home in a half-hour."

While Reg stayed there on her porch, smoking her cigarettes, Sarah Lee made her way over to the bus stop on the corner. You couldn't tell by looking at her, but her left leg was a quarter of an inch shorter than her right. She always stood a bit askew, one leg in front of the other, her hips cocked. It meant popping joints, bones that rattled, and a constant painful kink in the muscles of her lower back. But like Tal's leaving—or her ex-father's, for that matter—it was a pain so familiar she'd forgotten it was there, forgotten why she walked the way she did. It was what she woke up to every morning. Only that.

Once, before Ry was born, Tal had taken her to Mexico. She'd sat on the hood of a cherry-bright rental car as heat lightning pulsed in great white spasms over the Pacific. Tal kneeled on the hot parking-lot asphalt, prostrating himself before her, kissing her feet and ankles. Later they sat in their hotel's beachside bar, sipping sweet rum drinks from crockery cups. No one expressed concern as the hillsides bracketing Manzanillo Bay burned. They asked their waitress and she shrugged without looking at the fires and said only, *the farmers*.

The difference between that life and this one made her feel hollow inside.

Sarah Lee caught the bus and took it four stops to a soccer field, which was still soggy with the melting of yesterday's snow. She walked across the field and through the playground to the school's back door, joining a couple of dozen other parents and caregivers when the bell sounded.

The door was opened by a teacher, who looked for each child to recognize an adult before releasing them into the world. The children's exposure to an adultless world lasted for only a heartbeat, and then they were back in the care of a grown-up. It reminded Sarah Lee of a trapeze act.

Before dinner, she sat on the sofa with a can of hard iced tea while, at her feet, Ry plugged Lego bricks into one another, building a house for his noisy little battery-operated hamster. He was blond as beach grass, with large, wide-set hazel eyes, and he looked so much like Tal—in the shape of his face, and his mouth especially—that it sometimes hurt her to look at him. When a smile broke across his face, it gave her a feeling like a mouthful of sweet wine, sharp and warm in her cheeks.

She went out to the porch to have a cigarette. Reg was still out there, his legs crossed on one of the wire chairs, using the lid of a jar of jam as an ashtray. Beneath the lid was a pack she figured to be hers.

"That my spare pack?"

"Yep. I'll get you back. Next trip to the store."

"Me or you?"

"I'll take a walk in the morning."

"Thought you couldn't walk that far. Isn't that the whole issue?"

"Can't stop altogether. Everything'll lock up."

She took the chair next to him and held her hand out. "Give 'em here," she said, and he passed her the pack. She took one out, ran it under her nose to sniff the paper and the tobacco, then popped it in between her lips. Reg retrieved a Bic from the front pocket of his shirt and flicked, holding the flame out toward her.

The clouds piled up on the horizon as the afternoon pinched toward evening, arranging themselves into shapes like a map of lost continents cast in bronze. The air around them held a sweet April dampness, looked and felt green. Sarah Lee found herself drawn into a moment of dreaminess looking at the clouds.

"Beautiful," Reg said, having followed her eyes to the sky. He said it again, slowly, as though he had come across some archaic meaning of the word.

His voice brought her back to the porch, and to the man sitting next to her. The man who'd been her father until he decided, when she was almost exactly Ry's age, that he no longer wanted to be. She went looking for memories of him from back then, but she didn't find much. Just things she associated with him, tenuously, perhaps erroneously: instant coffee, Player's Navy Cut cigarettes, galoshes, an uncle who'd fiddled in Don Messer's Islanders, fields of corn, mumbled sermons. Alcoholism like an heirloom, passed down and down again. All just an approximation, something short of understanding. There was nothing she could hold on to.

For dinner she made pancakes in a skillet that still smelled of ground beef. "It's the only thing I can be sure he'll eat," she said to Reg, who sat hunched over in a chair in the middle of the kitchen, watching.

Over dinner, it grew into a gloomy evening, a mean fog blowing in off Lake Ontario. Despite that, Reg went back out to the porch to smoke, while she put Ry to bed.

"You need a bath," she said, tucking a fleece blanket over his thin chest and shoulders. His fingernails were dirty, his hair matted.

"No."

"In the morning. Remind me to remind you."

"Never never."

"Right." She kissed his forehead. "Right right."

On a shelf over his bed was half a wasps' nest, three rocks, three more pine cones, and an animal he'd made out of a toilet paper roll and yogourt cups.

She turned off the light.

"You worry too much over that boy," said Reg when she went back out to the porch.

"What the hell would you know about it?"

"I know, I know," he said, "you'll always have that comeback."

"It's not a comeback, Reg. It's just a fact. It's how things actually are."

"It's always something," he said. "I'm not perfect. Nobody is."

Sarah Lee said goodnight then and went to bed, where she seethed and watched TV until it was far too late to get a good night's sleep.

She forgot to put Ry in the bath the next morning, but managed to deliver him to the lineup outside the primary doors just as the bell rang. Then she took the bus to the central depot where Regina picked her up for their Tuesday houses. There were three of them in the Bridle Path, awful new houses with concrete statuary and pea gravel in soft pastel shades between the ornamental shrubs, extra cars in the long drives.

Regina was her sole confidante, a woman somewhere between thirty and death. Sometimes Sarah Lee thought Regina might be younger than she looked, which was not to say that she appeared haggard or worn, but rather that there was a kind of sturdy timelessness about her which made it seem improbable she had ever participated in the inconstant passions of youth. There was also her wisdom, dispensed like Tic Tacs from a bottomless clear plastic box always found at the bottom of her purse.

"He's my ex-father," she called from the bathroom, where she was wiping down a mirror. Regina was two rooms away, dusting, but there was nobody home, so they could be as loud as they wanted.

"Defrocked?"

"What? No, not a priest. He's my dad, but he walked out when I was six. He stopped being my dad when he did that. Ex-father."

"Oh, hon, I'm sorry," Regina said. "Okay, I'm turning this on."

Sarah Lee heard the vacuum switch on, Regina's voice swallowed up inside a vortex of whirring and sharp clicks as the suction plucked God knows what from the carpet's deep, rich fibres. They told clients they could clean a house so not even the police would know who'd been there, and sometimes Sarah Lee wondered if that's exactly what they were doing. The things she found.

Minutes later, when she'd finished the home-theatre room, Regina continued, "Bad house guests are the worst."

"It's so much worse than just that," said Sarah Lee, but then felt too tired and deflated to tell Regina just how bad it all really was.

When they got home, Ry racing so far ahead that he had to wait for her at the front door, they found that Reg was out. Sarah Lee felt happier than she'd expected to. The day had turned bright and warm. The apple tree which hung over the ratty and crooked fence from the neighbours' yard was thinking about coming into blossom. Ry had made it through the school day without peeing his pants.

She took a tall can of hard iced tea from the fridge, then she and her boy went out into the small yard, where she sat on the back step and watched him crawl around on his knees and hands, looking for treasures in the new grass. Nearby, somebody was playing a violin, music more beautiful than she could stand. She shut her eyes against it, wished they'd stop. What would anybody do with more happiness? She'd had more, once, and it left her limping and speechless. It slammed the door on her bare knuckles. Tal would've crawled over broken glass and rusted nails to put his nose against the softest part of her neck—and then, all of a sudden, he wouldn't.

Where's the comfort in something so fickle?

Ry found an earring in the grass. She got another iced tea. There was orange juice on the wall near the fridge, in sticky little dots, and the inside of the microwave was covered in a dull, oily sheen.

Where did all the hours of the day go?

Reg came home with fresh cigarettes and a nasty attitude.

"I got this pack, but I can't keep doing that. I have to think about the costs I'll incur once they slice open my leg."

"You and me both."

"You got more of those iced teas?"

"See, like that," she said.

"I think we should take a little trip. When's your next day off?"

"Sunday. Where?"

"See your mother."

Sarah Lee's mother, Betty Counsell, had been buried seven years. Betty was small and talkative, not exactly pretty but alluringly alive. There was a thickness in her consonants that always made Sarah Lee think of heavy, moist clay soil, of terrestrial concerns. Her mother was an earthy woman, an impression confirmed by every maternal relation Sarah Lee had ever met. They were earthy people.

Betty now rested in a small, cornfield-enclosed hillside cemetery in East Garafraxa, Ontario, the fecund nexus of Counsell family history. It was where Reggie Gallard, a lowly field hand, had fathered Sarah Lee before taking both her and young Betty to the rim of Toronto in order to dispatch taxis and sling burgers and cut grass and collide with police cruisers in a rusty Chevy Nova.

East Garafraxa had long assumed a note of whimsy in Sarah Lee's mind, tinged with as much inaccessible magic as its Seussian name suggested. The place was real, yes, but so removed from her. In East Garafraxa, there were crows the size of dogs, and waterways that froze solid so it was possible to excavate elaborate tunnel systems through them, and to live in those tunnels from Christmas until March, and children were conceived in the open tilled fields on orange summer evenings. In East Garafraxa, there radiated the disorienting sense that history had been made there, was still capable of being made there.

Something had ended just short of her, and now Sarah Lee and Ry were left doing whatever they would do in a vacuum, until they stopped doing it. And then they would just be gone.

The slim volume of her history was written within the rectilinear bounds of Ajax. She was an average child, happy until Reg's ghost routine, sullen afterwards. Whip-smart, or so said Betty. In high school, where her best friend was a girl named Alberta Milk, Sarah Lee was vampy and bold and did not for a moment suspect she was the freest she would ever be. Tal came then, as well as the tailspin which felt like an ascent—or velocity, in any case. Substance abuse, bad jobs, selfish sex. She was unable to see her youth's fast-approaching end, a future of precarious employment and damaging relationships, with a child but no mate, saying to anyone who'd listen, *How did I get here?*

Instead of creating new memories, she was merely existing. Her days were like tape unspooling from the mouth of a machine. The most solid thing she had was Ry's dependence on her. She had to keep him going. Try to expose him to happiness.

There was no place for Reg in all this.

"So let's go," he said again.

"I don't think so, Reg," she said.

"How come?"

"First thing is, in whose car? We don't have a car."

"I can see that."

"Second thing is, fuck you. You didn't care about Mom dying when she did it. Why would you care now?"

"Well, I just thought—"

"Nope, just realized I don't care. Whatever answer you're about to give, swallow it. I shouldn't have asked the question."

"Aw, you don't know what you want. Neither'd your mother."

"Do us both a favour and open up that pack of cigs and put one of them in your mouth," said Sarah Lee.

"I guess I will," said Reg, but he looked like he wanted to put a fist through some drywall.

Before anybody could say anything else, Sarah Lee stood and went in the back door, past Reg's daybed chamber and into the kitchen to see if she could find anything other than Kraft Dinner and boiled wieners to call dinner.

A few months earlier, Sarah Lee had opened her eyes and realized that Ry wasn't the round bundle she'd always known him to be. He was a rake. She was at a point where she was glad when he ate anything, and had taken to shovelling empty calories in any form into him in the hopes that he'd start to fill out. The nutritional value she didn't worry about; she had a blind sort of faith that his body would take care of all that. So the fact that he'd had seconds of the Kraft Dinner—with extra ketchup—felt like a bit of a victory. Possibly even enough of one to salvage the day.

She finished the dishes—Reg never offered—while the boy sat on the couch watching one more episode of *Paw Patrol*. Then she went out to the front porch, where Reg sat in silence. She could tell by his shoulders that their earlier conversation was over and done. They'd both forgotten it, or wordlessly agreed to pretend they had. That was fine by her.

"He needs a bike," Reg said. "How's a boy gonna explore his world without a bike?"

"Got one, but the tires are flat," she said, sitting down in the chair next to him and signalling for a cigarette.

He gave her the pack from his pocket. "We'll fix it," he said.

"Don't think they can be fixed," she said. "Needs new ones. You like to pay for that?"

"No."

"No, me neither."

"Should have maintained it. Kept it up. That's what you need to do," he said. "You've got to maintain the things in your life. It's the things we don't maintain that always come back to bite us in the ass."

Sarah Lee was about to say something in reply, something about how his statement was kind of rich, given their current situation, but then she saw that the bronzed continents of clouds were back high out over the lake, and the birds were in a state of uproar over something she couldn't glean.

She bent her head forward and pressed her chin to her chest, hoping to feel things lengthen and pop, to slacken the lacework of muscle strung between the shoulder blades, the spine as tent pole, holding even while bent against the weight. But she felt nothing, just a dry red heat in those muscles, the same old ache.

She decided she'd just let him have this one.

GRACELAND

CONNIE'D BEEN SICK about three years. When it became clear that she couldn't do it on her own, I moved back in. Her sister Georgia came back to Kemptville, too, and she brought her boyfriend Seb with her.

We'd been on again, off again for about ten years. Mostly on, but with some off periods, most of which were my doing. I told her early on, "I'm a sucker's bet." But then she got her diagnosis and everything kind of snapped into focus. After that, I put her to bed at night and I got her up in the morning and I stood outside the bathroom door when she showered, just in case. When I was working, Georgia would come by. It worked out because she served nights at the Breakaway and my shoots were all daytime gigs.

Every so often, if Connie was doing well, I'd wait until she was asleep, then slip out and drive the fifteen minutes into town to have a drink or two at the Breakaway. I could talk to Georgia there, which was nice. We could talk about Connie, even complain about her, and have everything be in bounds, because Georgia was the only other person in the world who really knew what my life was like. It was good to have her around, even for all the trouble it later brought.

Seb, on the other hand, I had my doubts about. He was lazy. He'd started three different courses of study, one at York and two at community colleges, and finished none. He'd been a carpet cleaner and a bouncer and a sandwich artist. After he and Georgia relocated from Toronto, the best he could find was overnights at a gas station. He made my spotty employment history look like the CV of a Fortune 500 CEO. He wore stupid jeans and he shaved his head twice a week and he listened to the worst music. "Club beats," he called them.

"What about Hank?" I once asked him.

"Hank who?"

That became our joke. Seb would have his music, which sounded like someone dropping a tennis ball down a laundry chute, playing on his phone, and I'd say, "Are you sure Hank done it this way?" And Seb would roll his eyes, and I'd laugh. If Connie was around, she'd howl, too. We did that bit all the time.

Once, Georgia suggested Seb help me with shoots.

"No," I'd said. "No way."

But she said, "Just try him out." And then she gave me those eyes, just like the ones her older sister used to give me—the ones I couldn't say no to.

Life walks on you when you're down. Hold that ruler against most any period of my life, and you'll see that was the size of things. But for a while there, things were fairly okay. I mean, Connie was sick and I was drinking, but I put a lot of trust in her doctors, who said a turnaround was possible. Money was coming in, and I was able to salt it away for whatever. Life was quiet in a way that seemed right, or anyway, appropriate to the circumstances.

Connie and I would sit in the house on Dennison Road and open a window. She'd light a joint, and I'd have something to drink. Before she got sick, we'd both have beers, but when things started to slide, it became a beer for me and a McDonald's vanilla shake for her. I'd hit the drive-through on 43 and speed back with it so when I got home it would be just soft enough but not all the way melted. After things got worse, she'd just sit with her joint.

In any case, we'd then turn on some music. Elvis, usually, but sometimes Bill Monroe, or Willie, or Waylon, or Hank, or Merle. Those were our guys, with Elvis at the top of the pyramid. Elvis before he got drafted, mostly, when he was just that Memphis mama's boy with a hickwise rumble in his getalong.

One night, when I was feeling flinty—the slightest little thing would hit me and break off little bits of my armour— Connie, out of nowhere, went, "You gotta take me to Graceland before I go, babe."

I said, "Naw, I'll take you to Graceland to celebrate when you get better." Then I had to leave the room so she wouldn't see that I was crying.

But most of those nights there'd be no tears. We'd get the music going, and I'd drink and she'd smoke, and we'd laugh. After putting her to bed, I'd pour myself some rye, a double, and put that back pretty quick. Often I'd have another—a triple. Then I'd fall asleep on the couch. In the morning I'd clear the fog with half a pot of coffee, before getting Connie up and fed and medicated.

Then it'd be time to care for my units.

My first was a Scout. I really only got it for hobby purposes. Back then I was mostly doing weddings, as well as a few small local contracts: brochures for a funeral home, a florist, a website for a dentist who'd just set up shop in a strip mall by the highway. I was getting by, but just.

At some point, I'd heard about people using UAVs to take photos, and that dovetailed beautifully with how much I loved playing with RC cars as a kid. I used to tape the family Handycam to the top of a 1:8 scale dune buggy and send it over jumps. Dad was less than enthused about that, but it was hard to argue with the results. One time I pointed it sideways and had some friends keep pace on their bikes. That was pretty impressive. "Like a real movie," Dad said, before he clapped me on the ear because he noticed the lens was scratched.

So I ordered the Scout. The moment UPS delivered it, I tore it open and plugged it all in to charge it. Maiden flight was in the yard, just to get some practice under my belt. It was a scorcher of a day, mid-June, high blue sky.

Connie, who'd been sleeping, wandered out onto the deck and found me hovering the thing ten feet off the ground, out above where the septic bed made the thick grass a deep, rich green. "Looks good," she called.

"Thanks. You're looking pretty good today, too." She still had her hair then, looked like she could put on a blazer and go stand behind the bank counter again. "Feeling okay?"

"Oh, you know," she said, and waved her hand around like she was conducting the youth orchestra. "Tired."

And it was true that she was kind of drawn in, a bit frail— but it was nothing like how she came to look later on. Before long, her hair would be gone and her skin would look like a shirt she'd been wearing too long, her eyes like someone had pressed their thumbs too deep into something gone bad.

After I'd practised manoeuvring the Scout a half-dozen times, I packed it in its black case, put it in my truck, and drove it down the road to where the Rideau's South Branch cut under Dennison. I relaunched my new toy in a clearing, got it up to about fifty or sixty feet before having it swoop down the creek and back.

The HD images coming over my tablet were some of the most beautiful things I'd ever seen. A smooth, clean, panoramic view of the green earth, the bending brown creek, and the horizon stretching toward the trees. It was more real than real, and in that moment everything clicked home. My jaw must have hit my knees.

Here it is, I thought. *My future.*

I flew the Scout around for another twenty minutes, zipping it over my head, doing enormous figure eights. It was a gorgeous, cloudless day. The sound of the rotors as it got near—a purring, seductive whirring—might as well have been the sound of my heart. Soaring, dipping, climbing, veering. Then I brought it in, landed it smoothly, and pointed the truck home to share my new excitement with Connie.

I found her on the bathroom floor, puking her guts out.

In short order, I'd set myself up as the go-to guy for aerial photography in Eastern Ontario. This had everything to do with my early adoption. I didn't need a helicopter. I had a helicopter in a suitcase. You wanted high-quality aerial footage of an event or location? Call Kirk Bedell. Tell me your needs and we can talk rates.

I got a call from Richard Aiello, a real estate guy who did a lot of high-end properties. He was based in Ottawa but would take listings from all over.

"I have properties that photos don't help," he said. "I need something bigger."

"You want video?" I said.

"I want you to use your little airplanes to get something amazing. I want blockbuster visual drama. I want people to watch a video and say, *I have to live there*."

"I can do that," I said. Then I had to figure out how to do that.

We—Georgia, Seb, Connie, and myself—were sitting around the kitchen that night over the remains of a pizza. I told them about Aiello's call.

"So what are you going to do?" Georgia asked.

"I'm going to meet him and I'm going to take all kinds of video of wherever he wants me to take video."

"Okay."

"Then I'll edit it."

Seb said, "Do you know how to do video editing?"

"No," I said, "do you?"

Seb shook his bald head like a big, dumb Lab.

"Well," I said, "figure it out and you've got a job."

And I will be damned if Seb didn't figure out this video-editing thing fast, and well. Georgia lent him some money for a new laptop, and he got some software for it, then he sat me down and showed me what he'd done with stuff he'd scoured off YouTube.

"Seb, seriously? You did this?"

"Yeah. You like it?"

"You're hired."

Aiello had us meet him at some million-dollar hobby farm near Merrickville. Forty acres or whatever, right on the river, fields and paddocks, big stone house, tree-lined drive. When we pulled up, he was standing next to his black Infiniti, feet spread wide. He was wearing a light blue polo shirt with his name and little personal logo on it. Black slacks, loafers. We shook hands, and the gold bracelet on his wrist jingled like sleigh bells. The skin on his face was soft-looking, like kid leather. He had these fleshy lips that he kept pursing and thick hands that he rubbed together, non-stop, as if he enjoyed the way they felt.

"This property has been on the market ten months," he said. "You're going to help me sell it."

"Sure thing," I said.

"Convey the grandeur," he said to me, raising his arms.

Seb unpacked and set up the Scout. I launched it whirring up into a perfect blue sky, then swooped it, taking long, gentle paths over the mature trees, across the fields, up the green, shaded lawn.

"That's a great toy," said Aiello.

The images coming in on the tablet were astonishing. It was like the opening shot of a Hollywood epic. Oscarworthy. I flew the Scout around and around. Walked slowly after it, awed by how beautiful and smooth it was as it buzzed around through the air, but trying not to let on just how amazed I was. Time passed quickly, and I really had no idea what I was doing. I figured, Kirk, you get a whole whack-load of footage, and then deal with it later. So we kept going and going, me balancing my fear that Aiello would see me as green against the fear that I'd miss something, some aspect or angle on the estate. I needed to hit a home run on the first try. I could see Aiello deciding to make this a regular thing, and I needed a regular thing.

Finally, after we'd shot and shot, I landed the unit and we packed up. Aiello shook my hand with his right while squeezing my shoulder with his left. He squinted and puckered his fleshy lips and said, "I can't wait to see it."

Seb and I sped back to the house and loaded the footage into his laptop's editing software. I hovered for twenty minutes and then Seb said, "Maybe you should go get us some beer. I think we'll want to celebrate."

I liked his confidence. "Okay. You have to do your thing. Is there anything I can do? Can I be useful here?"

"Tits on a bull," Seb said, and looked at me with his sad, brown eyes.

I made myself busy around the house for an hour. When I came back into the kitchen, Connie was standing behind Seb, looking over his shoulder at the laptop.

"Kirk, look at this," she said to me, without taking her eyes off the screen.

"Babe," I said, "you feeling okay? You shouldn't be standing so much."

"I'm great. Just look at this, will you?" she said.

"I'm not done yet," said Seb. "Don't get crazy until I'm done."

"Give the man room," I said to Connie. "Get in your chair, take a load off. I'll make dinner. How about carbonara? I know Spielberg here will be hungry."

The water wasn't even boiled yet when Seb said, "Done."

I crouched behind him. Connie shuffled in and stood behind me, put her hands on my shoulders for balance.

"You ready?" Seb asked.

"Yeah, yeah, play it."

He hit Play.

The video started with Aiello's name and logo and website, then faded into treetops racing by, shot from above. The music—I don't even know. If I'd heard that music anywhere else, I'd have hated it. There was a wash of fake strings and this bubbling sort of beat, like a drum machine had been thrown in a swimming pool. Horrible. But in context—with the shot rising over the trees and the house coming into view, its long drive snaking off-camera, then the tan metal roof, then the fields beyond, ending with a little sliver of the river—it was breathtaking. I mean that literally: the music took my breath. As though it had been composed for just that purpose. It made everything feel beautiful and urgent, and it made money feel insignificant, like I could just give everything I had to live in Aiello's stone house with that music piped in twenty-four hours a day.

"Seb, this music. Where'd you—I mean, you didn't make this music, did you?"

"No. Creative Commons, it's called. People make it and then give it away."

"Aiello's going to love this. He's going to lose his shit."

"I know."

He did.

Blood tests, blood tests, blood tests. New rounds of treatment. Glimmers of hope, setbacks, setbacks.

At one point, Dr. Parvinder said to us, "I think it's appropriate to be aggressive now."

"What the hell were we doing before?"

But Connie put her hand on my arm, like, "Whoa, relax. It's fine."

It amazed me how much faith she'd put in everybody there, all the doctors and therapists and nurses involved in her care. Higher forces, just about, for someone like Connie who'd never believed in God.

Living with someone going through this sort of thing can make you feel like a real little shit. Connie was heroic in the face of her illness, in a way that made me feel shame. There's no way I would've handled it like that. I knew it every day. Every time she shuffled into the room, laughing at a joke she'd just made, I felt dwarfed by her. Congrats, Kirk: you got the oil changed and made a dentist's appointment and remembered to buy cereal. Meanwhile she's managed to unearth the will to live yet another day in the face of horrendous pain and anguish.

The place near Merrickville sold. When Aiello called, he told me the buyer had specifically mentioned the video. "This relationship will be lucrative for the both of us," he purred.

I danced in place and pumped my fist and screamed silently while Connie, looking irritated, said, "What? What is it? Kirk, what?"

After I'd hung up, I said, "Babe, your man here just won the Super Bowl."

She smiled, then laughed a little, then started coughing and had to sit down.

That night, before I fell asleep, I asked myself if this was what success felt like. Then I asked myself if this is what happiness felt like. To both questions, I answered probably, at least a bit.

That new, totally unfamiliar feeling was related, I think, to my flying machines. Manoeuvrable, and outfitted with amazing little HD cameras, the UAVs gave me, for the first time, the ability to zoom in on things that were big and overwhelming. They said to me that, as long as I held steady, as long as I was true to my objective, I could analyze—and therefore come to grasp—big things as collections of little, understandable things.

And maybe get past them. The way Connie did.

Before, I would look at all the things ahead of us and

be completely overwhelmed by them, by the sheer stupid mass of what lay ahead of us, of her, and I would shut down. But she had a way of zooming in on each thing, of breaking it down to a bunch of smaller things that, each, on their own, were maybe manageable, were maybe things we could handle. A bunch of little tasks and way-points and easy objectives. *Just this appointment. Just this treatment. I'll be done throwing up in a few minutes.* It was a necessary way of looking at the world and saying, *We can do this.*

That's what the UAVs let me do, what drew me to them.

That and, you know, the money I was making.

After Aiello's call, we ate dinner. Then Connie sat in her big chair, put her feet up, and started taking all her evening meds, one by one. Blue ones, yellow ones, white ones, chasing each with a sip of water.

"What do you want to fall asleep watching tonight?" she asked.

The joke being that, though she was the terminal cancer patient, I was the one who always complained about being tired, the one who'd nod off in the middle of *Breaking Bad.* When Connie got tired, she'd just say, *I'm done*, then leave the room and go to bed—whereas I'd say, *I'm fine, wide awake!* before yawning really loud and then snoring like a bandsaw.

I said, "Whatever you want to watch is good."

Connie looked down at the remote, as if she wanted a firm plan in place before flipping on Netflix, to avoid that fifteen minutes of browsing that never leads to anything good.

And then she said, "I might need you to help me die."

"What?"

"You know," she said. "Come on. You know."

I looked down at my hands and said, "Okay, babe."

"If nothing else is working," she said, "you know."

"Yeah," I said, "I know."

My scalp went tight and my ears starting making a sound like strong wind.

"Don't worry. We can make it easy. Just a job that needs doing. A few things to tick off a list. You can handle it, babe. I have some ideas. Anyway, let's talk about it later. I can see it's freaking you out." She flicked on the TV. "You want to finish that *Lord of the Rings* one?"

"Sure," I said, forcing something sour and hot back down my esophagus and into my stomach, where it had started. "Perfect."

She'd opened the window next to her big chair a crack. A cold breeze slipped in, harbinger of fall. She lit up a joint. The movie started right where we'd shut it off the week before. There were pissed off orcs and translucent elves and the surround-sound clamour of swords clinking. Something screamed behind my head, then died. I was asleep in about twenty minutes.

The road south, after you crossed Beach Road—which was named not because there was anything resembling a beach anywhere nearby, but for the Beach family, Loyalists who'd had the first farm there—was called Rock Road, a rutted gravel lane with a mixed bag of tumbledown prefabs, trailers, and newer, swankier places. One of the latter was a three-storey timber-and-glass monstrosity that sat on top of a modest drumlin overlooking a pretty little meadow, a stone's throw north of Oxford Station, past where some hockey executive had a horse farm. It was on the market for two-and-a-half, said Aiello, meaning million, and it was our next project.

Seb and I headed there one early-December Saturday morning. The sky was cold and without end, and there was a light dusting of new snow. It was going to be a good day to shoot.

Seb, riding shotgun, was driving me crazy trying to play with the radio. At that particular moment, I was trying to listen to a show on NPR, floating up our way from Ogdensburg, New York, that played old country and hillbilly records on Saturday mornings. It was appointment listening for me.

"Fuck this inbred country shit," Seb said, as Jimmy Rodgers yodelled his way through "T for Texas."

"My truck, my inbred country shit," I said, slapping his hand.

"I'd like some more control," he said.

"Sure," I said, "next time we'll take your little Mazda 3, and we'll listen to all the DJ Dickie Duck you want, or whatever."

"I mean with the jobs. I was thinking that if I knew how to fly the units, we could do twice the jobs. You could expand the enterprise."

"Expand."

"Make more money."

Beautiful, stupid, brilliant Seb.

"I can teach you today."

The sun sparkled off the snow, and the sky was an eerie kind of blue. The timber-and-glass eyesore was dusted prettily, as were the majestic pines that surrounded it atop its little hillock. The whole thing looked like a diorama. Our breath streamed out of us in little white puffs. The air felt like a solvent, cleaning us out from our nostrils all the way down to our lungs, purifying our blood and making our brains' thoughts crisper, with hard edges that fit neatly together. I'm overselling it probably, but know this: it was a beautiful day.

Aiello trusted me enough now that he no longer showed up to shoots. That, plus the fact that the owners weren't home, made me feel at liberty to fuck around a bit and let Seb get his piloting feet wet.

I gave him a ten-minute tutorial, then turned the controls over to him.

Seb hovered the little copter at about head height for a moment, just looking at it, and then he had it shoot straight up into that endless sky.

"This," he giggled, "oh, this. This is awesome."

He made a few jerky stabs. The unit bucked and dropped slightly, then veered one way and another. Before long, though, he seemed to get the knack, and began carving swooping lines into the cold air over what looked like a horse paddock.

"This is awesome," he said again. "Like, really awesome." And he laughed like he'd gotten away with something.

"You're doing pretty good. I'll have to make you your wings. Little button. Maybe with tinfoil."

"'Licensed drone pilot.'"

"Co-pilot. You still have to log the hours."

"Fine by me. This is so cool," he said. Then, jerking his head toward the timber-and-glass building, he said, "So, are we gonna do this?"

I raised my arms above my head and said, "Convey the fucking grandeur, Seb!"

We got more footage that day, owing to Seb's greenness,

so it took a lot of extra editing. But in the end the video was pretty great. There were four offers and the place sold by Christmas.

While our bank accounts swelled, Connie shrank. It was like every time she coughed, some weight flew out of her. She could only sleep in little stretches, before waking up and moaning, pain running through her like electricity. I moved a cot into her room to be closer, so I could help when she needed me.

When you hear something like *I might need you to help me die*, you know, that's something that'll put you on your heels. But then she presented me with a checklist of small, easily accomplished tasks, and told me it would make the whole thing digestible, or doable:

Fill this prescription.
Buy syringes, some cut flowers, and that scented oil I like.
Run a bath.
Roll a joint.
Dry me off and dress me in a new nightie.
Blow dry my hair, set it in curlers.
Turn on the TV and let me watch something dumb while I
*   have that joint.*
Take the curlers out.
Bring me a mirror and let me do a bit of makeup
*   (not too much).*
Turn off the TV and play the CD with "Love Me Tender" on it.
Roll the bed out into the sunroom.
Open the windows.
Fill the syringe.

Sing along with Elvis to me.
Put the needle in my arm.
Give me a big kiss.
Say goodbye.

"See? Easy. You can do all that, babe," she said. "I know you can."

"Sure I can," I said.

But the next day, I went to the pharmacy and, instead of filling a prescription, bought a little vial of saline solution. What can I say? I never wanted to stop hoping things could turn out okay.

Time moved on two tracks over the winter. On the first track, professionally, things were great. Wonderful. I was getting jobs in Ottawa: commercial real estate listings, luxury homes, a big executive development with a golf course. Aiello's client list was swollen, and he wanted my help with just about all of them. I was conveying grandeur all over the place. I even ordered a night-vision camera to install on one of the units, with secret thoughts that I might use it to do something arty, or edgy, or weird, if there was a property that called for such a treatment. I was maybe entering my auteur phase.

The other track was winding and slow, uphill. Connie's health, trending downward. I was so used to her being skeletal and weak and discoloured that I couldn't remember the old Connie. She got through the winter but things weren't good. I could tell from the look on Dr. Parvinder's face, even if he kept saying the same things about *prudent courses of action* and *prognoses* and *promising new studies*, patting Connie's shoulder and reassuring her that she was remarkably courageous and strong and whatnot. We had a physical therapist who came to the house once a week,

Wednesday afternoons, a woman named Kat, and her tone of voice had changed from cheery to apologetic.

Some nights, I'd sit with my triple rye and wonder how I'd know when she was just about to die—or if Connie would know—and if she'd still ask me to do something about it beforehand.

We planned her birthday party anyway, because I guess it's important to have things to look forward to, even if you might not get there. Her birthday was May first. I always told her that if I knew anything about music, I'd write her a song called "May Day Baby." Empty words, since I was as useful with a guitar as I would have been in an operating room.

May first was a Friday that year, but Georgia couldn't get out of her shift, so we planned the party for the following night. The weather had turned beautiful. The crocuses were up and the spring peepers were out, making their noise. The air smelled earthy and felt soft. I'd bought nice wine and gone into Costco and picked up a bunch of little frozen appetizers and some big steaks to grill. Connie couldn't eat much but she said she wanted me to cut her thin little bits of good, rare beef.

"So thin it melts on my tongue," she said.

She would probably throw it up soon after, but before that she might feel like she'd indulged. I got her some fresh weed, too, and washed and ironed her green cotton dress, the only one that still fit her. We were going to do this right.

It was warm enough to have the windows open. I had some Hank on the stereo and I could hear birds. Connie was in bed, coughing and retching, but in high spirits. Seb and Georgia pulled into the driveway around four, and when they came through the door, I handed them each a gin and tonic in a tall, thin glass.

"Well, all right," Seb said.

"Where's the birthday girl?" asked Georgia.

"I'm in here, come in, Georgie," Connie yelled through the bedroom door.

Georgia walked down the hall. She knocked gently on the bedroom door, then hunched her shoulders to make herself small, opened the door a crack, and disappeared into the darkened room. There, I imagined, they began talking about sisterly things.

"Boss," said Seb. "The Cheap Executive Officer. What's our next gig?"

"Don't let's talk business now," I said. "I just want to enjoy the evening. You have to see these steaks I bought. Thick as a mattress."

"Delish."

"Oh, but okay, there's one thing. That night-vision camera came. I'm gonna put it on that black Phantom. We should play with that later. Very cool."

"Very cool. So, like, it takes good video at night? Does it use heat or something? Infrared?"

The jerk knew he could get me going if he asked about tech stuff, but I didn't want to get into it.

"I'll show you later," I said, putting the frozen hors d'oeuvres in the oven alongside the roasting potatoes. As I did so, I sang along with Hank: "I'm going down in it three times, but Lord, I'm only coming up twice."

Seb rolled his bulgy eyes. His freshly shaved head shone like a wet pearl.

The women emerged from the bedroom. Georgia held her glass in one hand and her sister's elbow in the other, taking her weight and helping her along. Connie was wearing the green dress, with a yellow scarf tied over her head.

I said, "Well, okay, here's the lady of honour!"

"Oh, jeez. Some honour," said Connie. "God, I wish I could have one of those G and Ts."

"Why not," I said.

"Come on," she said.

"No, really. I could mix you a little one. Just a splash of gin. It's your birthday, babe. Your goddamned birthday."

"What the hell," she whispered, as Georgia helped her down into a chair.

I sprang up and made her a drink before she could change her mind, and we all held our glasses in the air. "Happy birthday, May Day Baby," I said.

"Happy birthday to me," she said, and then brought the glass shakily up to her lips. She closed her eyes and sipped, wincing as she did. It had been a long time since she'd had a drink. "Hoo," she said once she'd swallowed. "Hoo, boy!"

We all sat around the table, the three of us nibbling on the hors d'oeuvres and putting back our drinks. Connie was smiling and looked happy, though tired. She sipped very slowly. The light was going outside.

I said to her, "What do you want to do, babe? What would make Connie happy right now?"

"I wanna play a round of Uno," she said.

"Great!"

I got the cards and we played and Georgia won. I fixed new drinks for everyone but Connie, who was still slowly making her way through her first. I made real howitzers this time, very generous pours. You could light these drinks on fire.

"You tell me when you want to eat," I said to Connie, "and I'll fire up the grill."

"Oh, whenever," she said. "I think I should move to my chair now, though."

It was true that she was looking a little run over—her colour had changed a bit, her eyes yellower and swimmy—so Seb and I moved her. Georgia brought her drink over and set it down next to the chair.

"I can't finish that," Connie laughed, which lifted my heart, to see that she was still trying to make things happy. "I'll save myself for the steak. I don't want the puking to start too early."

"Of course, hon," Georgia said, and whisked the drink away. I could hear the ice tinkling in the sink as she poured it down.

"How about I start up dinner now, then?" I said.

Connie nodded, pressing her thumbs into her eyes and sighing. It was taking a lot out of her. I thought, *Are we only pretending this is for her?*

"How about changing the music, too?" she said. We'd been listening to Hank all this time. "I've had my fill of the yodelling and all that."

"Sure, sure, of course. What do you want to hear?"

"Let's get some Elvis going."

"I'd love to," I said, and I put all the King's stuff on shuffle. I checked the potatoes before going out to fire up the barbecue. Then I brought out the steaks—four thick, bloody slabs of meat—and laid them across the grill, letting the hot flames just barely kiss the cuts before pulling them off.

Seb, who'd been standing quietly—reverently—next to me, whispered, "Nice."

We took the steaks inside, and Georgia handed us fresh highballs when we stepped through the sliding door. "Try this," she said, the ice cubes clinking and chiming like a swaying chandelier.

"What is it?"

"A Salty Dog."

"What's a Salty Dog?"

"Gin, grapefruit, salt."

"I'm into it," said Seb.

I sipped mine. Georgia had a beautifully heavy hand for an experienced server; the gin leapt up into my head and filled me with warmth and pale light.

We got Connie all settled in at the table. I opened the wine, pouring it into big, fat-bottomed glasses with delicate stems, then served out potatoes, salad, and the big cuts of steak. I sat down next to Connie and said, "How are you feeling? You need me to cut that up for you?"

The knives, which we almost never used, were these great bone-handled things that once belonged to her grandparents. The year before, I'd sharpened them so they could slip right through the toughest gristle. She picked hers up and turned it over in her skeletal hand, looking at her plate.

"Yeah," she finally sighed, deflating, "I guess I do."

I cut her the finest little slivers of steak and fanned them out for her in a pretty little pattern. "Potatoes, too?"

"I guess," she said.

When I was done, I looked up into her bruised face. She tried to smile for me but there was nothing behind it. She was on the way down, I could see. We had to hurry up and get this done.

She ate three of the little slivers, then put her fork down and said, sadly, "God, that was amazing."

Georgia and I finished our plates, and Seb went back for seconds of everything. Connie's wine was untouched, but the rest of us were ready for a refill. Things were just shy of jumping off the tracks. Seb did an imitation of me, a little hillbilly dance in the middle of the dining room with his hands on an imaginary belt buckle, throwing his heels out to the sides before finishing with a Vegas-period Elvis karate kick. There was a lot of laughing, and even Connie had tears in her eyes.

"Oh God, stop," she said. "You're gonna kill me." She rested both her arms on the table, out in front of her like the sphinx, and a peaceful look came over her. She tapped her brittle fingernails a couple of times and then said, "Is there cake? There better be cake."

"Ice cream cake," I said, and I pulled it out of the freezer. HAPPY BIRTHDAY, CONNIE, it read, in looping pink letters against the vanilla background. I put a pair of fake candles on it, little battery-operated LED tea lights, because I thought maybe the smoke would make her cough. We sang "Happy Birthday" and I put it down in front of her. She pretended to blow them out, then Georgia picked them up and flicked the little switches so they blinked off. I ran a big knife under hot water and carved off a slice for the birthday girl. She poked it, picked up a forkful, and put it in her mouth like she was testing it.

"Mmm," she said.

I served everybody else great heaping pieces. After, we all felt like stuffed and mounted game.

"Holy jeez, I'm full," said Georgia.

"I haven't eaten that much in months," said Connie. She sighed and patted her bloated belly. "And I won't do it again. What a party. But I'm feeling kinda flat. I better lie down for a bit."

"But the gifts," I said.

"Later," she said, waving her hand at nothing in particular.

"Later is perfect," I said.

Georgia went over and helped her sister up. Once Connie was standing, she came close, looked at me with misty eyes, and said, "Thanks, babe."

"Happy birthday, best girl," I said.

"I love you," she said in my ear, then wiped her leaking face across my shoulder.

"I love you, too."

Then Georgia led her down the hall and they disappeared into the bedroom.

"Goddamn," I said to nobody, feeling a stinging in my eyes. Seb put his big hand on my shoulder. "Yeah, yeah," I said. "Help me with these dishes."

When we were done, we opened beers and I led him outside. A light misty rain had fallen while we were eating, and the cool night smelled like frogs and worms. Seb—who I, at the moment, was feeling fond of in a fatherly kind of way—trailed after me as I went across the wet lawn and over the gravel drive to the garage.

The motion-sensor lights flared on when I opened the door, illuminating my lair. Deep metal shelves lined one wall, piled with UAVs and their parts, controllers, cameras, and the dense black plastic cases the units travelled in. On the adjoining wall was my workbench, a bunch of tools hanging from a pegboard, cords, power bars, and batteries plugged in, blinking. On the floor were six bigger drone units, like giant bugs at rest.

"Here's the night-vision," I said, pulling a small cardboard box with a shipping label down from a shelf. "Just came the other day. I haven't even opened it."

"So cool," Seb said, because he didn't know what else to say.

Installing it was a pretty simple matter. I pulled the black

Phantom 3's old camera out from inside a little protective cage on the bottom of the machine and popped the night-vision camera on.

"They design 'em to be modular like that," I said. "Gives the end-user greater freedom." When I'm drunk I like to talk about things like I know what I'm talking about, using words like *modular* and *end-user*.

"So cool," said Seb.

I powered the Phantom up. Everything seemed to be in good order, so I flipped off the lights in the garage. Seb and I appeared on the tablet I'd plugged into the controller, colours inverted, our eyes glowing in stray light like green fire. We looked like raccoons caught raiding a Dumpster.

"Holy shit," Seb said, "it totally works."

I rolled open the big garage door and the night came in, with its coolness and its smells and the wet grass catching bits of light like tiny polished jewels. I jammed my thumb up against the joystick, the four blades whirred to life, and the Phantom rose off the ground and into the air.

"Let's play with it a bit," I said.

A small flashing red light and a soft insect-like buzzing sound were the only indications that there was anything in the sky above our little bungalow, but the images coming back showed the house and everything around it in perfect, though skewed, detail. It looked like wartime news footage.

"See what the girls are up to," said Seb.

"Yeah, we'll give them a little scare."

I piloted the Phantom around back, maybe ten feet away from the eavestrough, and the tablet showed us the kitchen window, then siding, siding, the bathroom window, and then Connie's room. Inside, the ghostly image of Georgia sat on the edge of the bed while Connie, cheeks shining, spoke. We couldn't hear them, but I was certain they were seconds away from noticing the hovering machine outside the window, then maybe giving a little shriek before starting to laugh. But they didn't. They didn't see it. I held the unit steady with the joystick, and the image came back so still it was like it'd frozen in place. I zoomed the camera in.

Georgia took Connie's hand in hers, then began sliding her grip up toward the elbow. Her other hand came up then, and I could see it, plain as day. Weird and green, like it was radioactive, the syringe was small but unmistakable. There was no missing it.

They still hadn't seen the Phantom.

Connie's smashed-in chest rose and fell sharply, but she was nodding her head. Georgia took her hand off Connie's arm and tapped the syringe. Connie curled her fingers into a fist.

I pressed the controller's Return To Home button, handed it to Seb, and started sprinting toward the house. The UAV passed over my head on its way back to the garage. I shouted "Connie, no! No, babe!" as I ran into the house, scampered down the hall and into the doorway of her bedroom.

"What are you doing? You said. I was supposed to. Connie?"

They looked at me in the dim light of a lamp on the bedside table, their expressions shocked at first, but then Georgia's turned angry while Connie's slid into sadness.

"Shit," said Georgia. She rested her right hand on her right knee, still holding the syringe, then stared at Connie, waiting to be told what to do next.

"Connie? Babe?" I said. "What am I doing out here all day, Con? Why am I trying? You have to want it."

Elvis was still playing, back in another part of the house, but it wasn't "Love Me Tender." It was "Milk Cow Blues," which meant nothing to us.

"Oh Jesus, Kirk. Look at me."

She fixed me with this awful, pleading, watery stare, and in it I saw that all the things I'd dreamed had made me into a person who was worth something were, in fact, meaningless.

"What do you want me to say," she said. "You never could have gone through with it. I know that, and so do you."

I got all blubbery then.

She said, "Am I wrong?"

"No," I said between sobs, "you're not wrong."

"Babe," she said tenderly, "you never even took me to Graceland."

FOOTWORK

MOST DAYS, CLAUDIA'S GRIEF was indistinguishable from joint pain: hard and stubborn and debilitating. It denied her the ability to plant firmly, and was softened only a shade by food, sleep, or wine. She wondered if *grief* was even the right word for what she was experiencing.

Bo wasn't dead, he'd just left. On January third. Left her and left their little cabin in the woods, where she thought, in better days, they would ride out eternity, or at least their little share of it. But he'd found it—and her—lacking, so he got into his car and was gone. Gone to the big city, or to another town, or to wherever men go when they decide they don't have what they want.

There are new stakes, she said to herself then. Her life felt like it had suddenly become very open and stark, and everything she did would in some way be a preparation for death, whenever it might come. So she did very little. She was paralyzed. She lost weight and her hair began to thin. She found it in the sink and the shower, and on her pillow.

Claudia spent the rest of the winter in bed, more or less, and when spring came, she barely registered it. Only the new sweetness of the light made an impression on her, its strength, its proximity. But she didn't do the regular spring things. She planted nothing. She maintained nothing. Every day her little cottage fell a little closer to its ruin, and she did nothing to slow its collapse. There were little seedlings—maple and tamarack and oak—peeking up over the lip of the eavestroughs. There were mice in the cabin's walls, and rot in its window frames, and the stovepipe needed cleaning before the next winter came. But she couldn't muster the resolve. She just couldn't.

She worked days in a coffee shop called the Fresh Start, on the crumbling brick edge of the shabby town twenty kilometers away. Train cars full of oats and molasses rumbled slowly by, twice a week, on their way to the big sweet-smelling factory by the river, where they made granola bars that were then shipped out by truck. You could smell it all over town, the aroma floating up the river toward where a big, thick forest used to stand. On Mondays and Tuesdays, the factory made chocolate chip bars. On Wednesdays, strawberry. Blueberry on Thursdays. Claudia didn't know what the factory did on Fridays, and she assumed nothing happened on weekends. She couldn't know for sure, though, because she spent her weekends at the cabin.

Before Bo left, their weekend routine involved sleeping late, keeping busy in the afternoons with upkeep and projects, and then either roasting a chicken for dinner or slow-cooking a thick soup to eat with bread she made in a machine that whirred and churned and hopped across the counter. As the light slipped away they would play cards on the porch or drink wine and watch television, and then make love with the windows open. She didn't know why Bo had wanted to leave that. Unless there was just something particular about her that he no longer cared for.

Life was taking on a restrictive shape now, narrowing toward an end which she could feel with awful certainty.

Across the street from the coffee shop was an old brick building. Viewed from above, it was shaped like an H, its two long, narrow wings joined in the middle by a brick wall, cut at the centre by an archway just wide enough to fit a sedan through. It had been built early in the previous century to house weaving machines, was later fitted to accommodate the manufacture of transistors, then had a third life as storage for the larger electronic-components plant across the street, and was finally sold off when the owner of the big plant moved most of its operations to Mexico.

The new owners eventually chopped the H-shaped building up into discrete units and leased them out. Now there was a welding shop, a rock-climbing gym, a fairtrade coffee roastery, warehouse space, and a fencing and archery club.

One October morning, Claudia pulled into the Fresh Start's pocked lot and spied the fencing club's sign in her mirror.

Maybe I ought to try something I've never had an interest in trying, she thought.

And just like that, something fell into place.

For months, because there was so little left in her life that she cherished, she felt untethered. Only now, for the first time, did she see that as a form of freedom.

She was going to be forty in a year. She didn't particularly feel like making a big deal out of the aging milestone. Lordy, lordy. Nor did she want to stake her self-improvement to what amounted to a pretty arbitrary date. But neither did she feel much like wallowing any longer. Love, money, red wine, loneliness, insomnia. She had been pulling the memory of Bo—the shame of having him walk out on her—like it was a tractor tire fixed to her waist with a length of zinc-plated chain, and the weight of it all, on her neck and shoulders, was tiring.

She was tired of waking up tired.

Claudia had a reservoir of strength. She'd been avoiding it, but it was there. Strength and anger. After the divorce, when she was five, she'd been raised by her mother, Gloria, her father having essentially disappeared. When Gloria taught Claudia to play cards, she told her that the queen was above the king. Anything which required doing, said Gloria, was best done yourself. Gloria met life with tenacity and not a little bit of animosity.

Surely to God, Claudia had access to that resolve? Atop all the other things she'd inherited, including, likely, a susceptibility to breast cancer? It seemed only fair.

Claudia had dated a fencer in her last year of high school, a floppy-haired boy named Will who was bound for Queen's University, and for tournaments at Ivy League schools, and for an MBA and unqualified happiness. He was a lousy kisser, though, which justified her decision to dump him just before finals. But before dumping him, she'd watched him fence two or three times, and because of that she felt she understood the rudiments of the sport.

Claudia rolled her little hatchback into the Fresh Start's parking lot, fifteen minutes early for her shift. She stepped out of the car, standing taller than she'd done all that summer. The vertebrae between her shoulders popped and stretched out. She could feel the tissue between them grow spongier. Then she walked across the street, carried on pistoning legs, to the big metal door of the South End Fencing and Archery Club, and was happy to find it unlocked.

That night, Claudia baked a uniquely aromatic loaf of bread and cinnamon buns, for nobody but herself. As she baked, she waggled a hot cinnamon toothpick in her mouth, of the sort she always chewed while baking so she wouldn't be tempted to eat too much of the food she was preparing. She was introduced to them as a young girl, during one of her mother's semi-annual attempts to quit smoking. Claudia had used them ever since, and not just as an appetite suppressor. They were also an anxiety aid, and likely the reason she'd never started smoking in the first place.

Unfortunately, the hot cinnamon taste now reminded her of Bo. Specifically, it reminded her of one afternoon at the end of a long drive through Vermont. They'd found themselves in a small valley among low mountains, where a shallow river—almost a creek, the water clear and cold—wound around a ball field and a church and a creamery. They stopped the car and went down into the creek bed, pulled off their shoes, rolled their jeans up to their knees, and waded into the water. She remembered they had to step lightly on the bottom, lined as it was with rocks of grey and pink and white, granite and shards of pottery and glass, fragments of bricks stamped or chiselled with the names of manufacturers long gone. It was as if the cold clear water had swept the physical material of history to that spot, under their feet, and preserved it for that very afternoon. They had stood in that water beneath the high blue melancholy sky, the air humming about them with dragonflies and heat, the water so cold that it sent a pain up through their legs and trunks into their teeth and foreheads, and they kissed, and she tasted cinnamon on his lips, and he tasted it on hers, because during the drive they'd chewed through a whole package of the toothpicks, chewed them so long their lips stung.

They were, back then, more in love than anyone had a right to be. Those days came back to Claudia now, as she chewed every toothpick until it was frayed and splintered and she had to replace it with another from the little box. But the memory didn't bite the way most of them had in the months since he'd gone. Instead, in the warm, moist, bread-scented kitchen, she was buoyant. Her first fencing class was coming up, and it had been so long since she had done something new that her scalp felt as tight as a drum.

Claudia had three glasses of wine, slept poorly, and rose excitedly in the morning. Eight hours at the coffee shop, then she'd eat a dinner of odds and scraps from the kitchen, and just before six-thirty she would change into sweats and cross the street and walk into a new thing. She took the feeling in her stomach—of motion and unease—as a good omen.

At the entrance to the fencing club, the man who'd registered her and taken her cheque the day before—Arthur, she thought his name was—was standing with his back to the door, hands clasped behind him. His brown hair was thin and close-cropped, and he wore black: black polyester track pants, a black pullover, black Nikes. When the door clanged shut behind Claudia, he turned around.

"Hello again," he said, smiling. "Glad you could come."

"Well, this is what I signed up for, right?"

"You're nervous. Don't be nervous. We'll get started in a few minutes. Have a seat there and change shoes."

There was a mania about the shoes, she'd noticed. NO OUTDOOR SHOES signs were placed immediately inside the door, and then at regular intervals along the wall, and there was one taped to a placard on a stanchion planted between grey plastic boot trays.

She sat on the long bench beneath coat hooks and faced the large room's focus and purpose: a dark, rich wooden floor, raised slightly, just a step, above the painted concrete beneath her feet. There were eight lanes—*pistes*—painted across it, from her left to her right. Between the pistes were padded columns that reached up to the ceiling, maybe fifteen or sixteen feet high, iron trusses beneath planks of wood painted white sometime in the last century and not once since. Archery targets lined the far wall. Nearer to her, on the left, was a whiteboard. Opposite that, bracketed by two large rolling doors which opened, she figured, to the parking lot, were racks of equipment: foils below, clasped at their bell guards, tips pointed downward; above, two neat rows of masks, like blank faces.

There were seven other people in the room besides Arthur, all of them pulling up, strapping on, and tying various pieces of apparel and equipment. It was clear they knew one another, as they milled and lounged and snarked at each other beneath the archery targets. Claudia removed the dowdy but supportive white Reeboks she wore at the coffee shop, pulled her cleanest running shoes from her gym bag, and slipped them on.

In the waiting area to Claudia's right were four doors, all now open. Three led to small change rooms; the last, nearest the gym floor, opened to an office, into which Arthur disappeared for a moment. When he came back out, he was wearing a thick black jacket, like a smock, over his pullover, and a black mask cocked back on his head so that his face was visible.

"Okay, everybody, let's meet over at the board," he said.

The congregants made their way to the whiteboard and arranged themselves in a semicircle. Claudia finished tying her shoes and went over to join them, stepping up onto the beautiful floor and feeling its firmness and flex beneath her feet.

They were anywhere from fifteen to forty, the fencers. Two or three wore simple sweats, like her, but most wore the white breeches with suspenders and long socks she always associated with fencing. There was only one other woman, who looked to be about thirty. The rest were boys and men, which she thought she should have anticipated, but hadn't.

"Okay, folks, this is Claudia. She's starting with us tonight."

Claudia nodded, smiled shyly, said, "Hello," and was met with apparent indifference. She wondered if there was a general tendency for new people to burn out quickly.

"We'll focus on strength tonight," said Arthur, "but we'll also get some fencing in toward the end. Domenic, you'll lead the warm-up. Evelyn, why don't you stick with Claudia to help her through what she might not know."

"Sure," said the other woman.

"Okay," said Arthur, "let's move."

The group broke quickly, like startled animals, and began running around the floor's perimeter in a counter-clockwise circle.

As they jogged, Evelyn came abreast of Claudia and said, "Hi."

"Hi."

"We'll do a few laps like this and then start the stretching."

"Okay."

"Just watch me."

After four laps around the gym, which had Claudia feeling the limited capacity of her lungs and rib cage, Domenic called for them to begin: "On toes!"

The runners immediately rose up onto the balls of their feet, with their arms stretched above their heads. Claudia watched them a moment, unsure that she was seeing what she was seeing. Evelyn nodded to her and said, "Like this," and together they tiptoed around the gym stretched as long as they could get, reaching for the ceiling.

Then Domenic said, "Sweeps!"

Sweeps turned out to be long strides where the torso would be held straight and upright as a church pew, the front leg bent at the knee at, or close to, ninety degrees and the trailing leg almost touching the floor. With each step the fencers would brush an arm down, low enough to sweep the floor with their fingertips, before bending the elbow and bringing both hands up to shoulder height to meet at the chest, in a small gesture that looked like prayer. On the next awkward step forward, they'd repeat the sweeping motion with the other hand.

Claudia watched Evelyn closely for two or three repetitions, and then she did her best to mimic the motion, feeling the muscles of her hips strain and flex and then open up. She completed a circuit of the gym, losing her balance two or three times along the way. But she liked the feeling, liked the strangeness of it. How, at the bottom of the exercise, she felt like she was supplicating. She liked, above all, the arcane nature of it, how she was like an adherent to something secret, with its own language, costume, and rites. She was glad she had chosen this, whether accidentally or by providence, as a means of rejoining her body—her life. Had things gone only slightly differently, she might at this very moment be in a spin class instead.

After the warm-up, the others began running wind sprints, from end line to warning line to end line to on-guard line to end line to centre line, and so on. Arthur called her aside to begin her introductory lesson. First, he handed her a binder.

"This is your textbook," he said, putting it in her hands. "Don't be intimidated. It's history and rules, as well as techniques. It has questions to help you study. There's everything you need to know to achieve your first arm-band in there."

"Okay."

"But that's later. Don't worry about it now." He smiled, the brown bristles of his goatee encircling his mouth. "I'm freaking you out, aren't I?"

"No," she said. "Yes."

"Really, don't worry about it. Just take in what you can tonight and come back next week and we'll start to work."

"Okay," she said, "yeah."

"Now," he said, "if I were to say *Smirnov* to you, what would you think?"

"Vodka?"

"Right, that's what most people say."

"But no?"

"Smirnov was a Soviet fencer, early eighties. He died. Opponent's foil went right through his mask, into his eye, right in his brain." Arthur used the index and middle fingers of his right hand to mimic the blade's course through Smirnov's mask and into his eye.

"Jesus."

"But he's the reason we have all this," he said, patting his jacket with one hand and pulling on his mask with the other, his voice warm and muffled. "Caused a whole rethink of the protective equipment. We're safe because of Smirnov. That's how I think of it. Everything was reconsidered."

"Oh, well, that's good."

"Right? So okay, the mask," he said. "The screen over your face has to be able to hold more than fifty pounds. Let's get you one." He led her to the rack on the wall and took down a headpiece of heavy cotton and plastic and black metal screening, and said, "Pull it on."

She tightened her ponytail and slipped the mask over her head. She was surprised at how well she could see through the screen. It appeared nearly opaque from the other side.

"How's that?"

"Feels good," she said.

"Yeah. Pretty soon that's how you'll see the world. When you're not wearing one, you'll wish you were."

He took her to a room off the office and showed her the rest of it: the jacket; the underplastron, which was a half-vest worn under the jacket to protect the underarm and the side of the fencer's chest nearest their opponent; the glove; and the hard plastic chest protector. And then the foil, with its perfect balance and its pistol grip. He handed her one and she weighed it, pushed its tip into the floor and felt the blade tense and bend.

"Go ahead," Arthur said, holding his fingers like a gun and thrusting them out.

She extended her arm and leaned forward, twisted her wrist around, made a circle in the air. It was so light, so comfortable in her hand.

"Yeah?" said Arthur, smiling, nodding. He rummaged through shelving in the large closet space for pieces of equipment to fit her, and said, "These are yours as long as you're here."

A sort of pride bloomed in her cheeks and the backs of her hands.

Later, at Arthur's suggestion, she sat cross-legged on the floor with a mask in her lap and watched the others practise. She saw how beautiful it was: a weaponized dance, improvised and ecstatic. The floor thumped with footfalls, white silhouettes racing back and forth in unison as though joined by invisible girders.

"Distance," Arthur called to the fencers, "remember your distance!"

On the nearest piste, Evelyn was fencing Domenic. Domenic was short and powerful-seeming, with no hair, but flecks of grey in his stubble, and round cheeks. He smiled with the warmth of a church on a winter night. Evelyn was sharp-featured, but not unfriendly, with light brown hair that looked dry and crinkly, a slight wave to it as it swept back into its ponytail.

Beforehand, Claudia had watched them gear up to fence with electronic scoring. They plugged wires into the backs of their lamé vests, wires which led back to pulley wheels suspended from the ceiling, then looped back to the scoring unit: a rectangular box, the size of an open lectern bible, with a square cluster of lights at either end. They tested the gear by pushing the points of their foils into each other's torsos. Then they donned their masks, stood on their respective

on-guard lines with their heels together, saluted with something like chivalry, and crouched into their stances.

Arthur, who stood off the piste near the centre line, said,
"Fence."

Domenic charged first, his wide, bouncy thighs hammering faster than Claudia's eyes could see. He went up on his
toes and exploded forward like a crane, but Evelyn deflected
his blade, spinning it to her side, then jabbed her foil into
Domenic's chest just below his mask, the foil curving until it
was nearly bent double. The cluster of lights nearest her end
flashed, and the bible buzzed its little sermon. Arthur held
up his right fist, the hand nearest to her. "Pointe," he said in
a clumsy French accent. "Excellent parry riposte, Ev."

The fencers crouched back into their on-guard positions.
"*En garde*," said Arthur. "*Prêt. Allez.*"

Domenic jolted forward again, bouncing like a Super
Ball, leaning forward, feigning jabs, leaning back. Evelyn
backed up, sliding one foot and then the other, until she
was nearly against the end line. She thrust defensively, a
bit desperately. Domenic weaved his head back and to the
side, before dropping low and lunging forward, propelling
his foil into Evelyn's stomach. The lights, and the buzz.
Arthur's left fist in the air. They walked back toward the
centre line, Evelyn with her head hung a bit, her ponytail
tufted out behind her.

Domenic scored the next five points. Then the alarm on
Arthur's phone buzzed, meaning they'd been at it for three
minutes, and they both stopped cold.

Arthur said, "Okay, salute."

The two stood again at their guard lines with their heels
daintily pressed together at right angles. They then tucked
their masks into the crooks of their left arms, held their foils

first up to their noses, then swept them down and away, and finally walked forward to exchange an awkward left-handed shake at the centre line.

"Grab some water," Arthur said, and they reached for bottles at the base of the column supporting the scoring box. "Ev, okay, great bout. Your lunge was great. I want you to watch your recovery. Keep it small, keep it controlled. Overall, good."

"I was on my heels too much," she said. "I couldn't generate any priority."

"Okay, how were your feet? Domenic's older than you, and he's breathing harder. Look at him, he's huffing and puffing. What does that tell you? How are you going to beat him?"

"More footwork," said Evelyn, her tone rising; a test balloon.

"More footwork," said Arthur.

There was a jagged physical sensation in Claudia's chest. The compass rose of her heart swung around, recalibrating. She was in bright company, feeling the sweaty sense of inclusion, a combative conviviality.

Hung on the wall, above the foils and masks, were four heraldic crests: wooden shields painted in blocks of red, white, yellow, black. Anonymous iconography suggesting loyalty to a team or nation she had never known. In that nation, citizenship required willingness and effort, and actions were recognized.

Claudia had found a home.

She ate little that night, her body tense and vibrating with new information. Since January she'd been trying to answer just one question: could she be happy alone?

Prêt. Allez. Parry, riposte, parry, lunge, point.

She ordered a cord of firewood the next day, and two weeks later, when it came tumbling out of the delivery truck's tilting bed and onto her gravel driveway, she stacked it herself.

The snow came early that year. It began when it got dark on Halloween night, the incandescent light in that part of town bestowing a strange violet haze, glittery and kind of frothy. Claudia got a little lost to herself looking at it out the window of the Fresh Start. It was a Monday, and the air smelled like chocolate.

Ten minutes before her shift was done, the door rang its bloopy electronic tone—she'd have preferred an actual bell, but the owner liked this doodad, which also counted the number of times the door opened—and Evelyn from the fencing club came in, unwrapping a scarf from her face and shaking snow out of her hair.

"Claudia," she said. "Hey!"

"Oh, hey, Evelyn," said Claudia, "how are you?"

"A bit low, you know? Could use a coffee before I get going over there."

"You change nights at the club?"

"No, I'm there two nights a week. Sometimes three, if I can do it."

"No trick-or-treating tonight?"

"No. It's just me, so nothing like that."

"Yeah, me too."

"You should come in an extra night. Mondays are good."

"Maybe I'll do that."

"So, this is where you work, huh?"

"This is me."

Evelyn took in the mint-green tabletops, the off-off-white counter, the foggy plate-glass windows, the three patrons, and the one other employee, a grad student named Leanne, who relieved Claudia three nights a week, and in whom Claudia saw herself from fifteen years earlier.

"Looks like a nice place to work," said Evelyn.

"A profoundly rewarding career choice," said Claudia.

"Oh, whatever. I'm twenty-eight and I work in a call centre," Evelyn said, and laughed.

"Same difference, I guess."

"I guess."

"Coffee. You want it to go?"

"You know what, maybe I'll sit a minute." She took the nearest chair, pulling it from beneath the table that Claudia had wiped down just a moment earlier.

Claudia picked up the coffee pot with the black rim and filled a mug to within a quarter inch of the lip. Evelyn then tore open two sugar packets and, pinching them together, poured the contents of both into the cup.

"So, fencing twice a week," Claudia said. "That's a commitment."

"It used to be five."

"Seriously?"

"It was kind of my thing."

"I guess it must have been. I can't do anything five times a week. I mean, I show up here, but only because I have to."

"I had it in my head that I was gonna make it to the Beijing Olympics. I'm goal-oriented. If I couldn't make Beijing, I was gonna be in London. Or die trying, I guess."

"Did you?"

"Nope. Wrecked my knee falling off a bike. Guy opened his door and I went right into it. Surgery. It was a mess. I didn't pick up a foil, didn't put on a mask, for eight years."

"Jeez. But you went back to it."

Evelyn nodded. "You know how maybe there's one thing in your life where you feel like you have some control? I guess it was that. I had to go back to fencing so the rest of my life wouldn't feel so scattered." She looked away from Claudia, down at her mug. She picked it up and blew on it, had a scalding sip, then tore the foil off the top of a little cup of two percent milk and poured it into the coffee.

"I don't think I have that one thing," said Claudia, still holding the coffee pot aloft, her other hand on her hip.

"I didn't know I had it until I didn't have it."

"Maybe I should start getting rid of things until I figure out what I have."

"Ha! Maybe that'll work!" Evelyn took a long sip of her coffee.

"You want more?"

"Nope. Gotta go. I have to go fence some teenage boys now. If you come Mondays, I can fence you instead." She laughed again.

"If only to spare you from that fate."

"Seriously," said Evelyn. She stood and put a toonie on the table. "That cover it?"

"Yeah."

"Okay. Thanks. See you Thursday night?"

"You will."

And Evelyn was back out into the snowy night, trudging across the street and into the old brick building.

That night, while the snow continued to fall, a black bear tripped the motion-sensor floodlight outside the back door of Claudia's cabin. The bear, likely in a state of panic—round and shiny, it would soon be going into hibernation—had found its way into some food scraps in the garbage, in the shed she'd mistakenly and uncharacteristically left unlatched.

Claudia pulled aside her curtains and watched its long claws tearing through the flimsy dark green bag. Then she lay back in bed listening to it grunting and banging. Continued listening, after it stumbled away, to the great silence, the snow still falling and insulating the world. It hummed below, throbbed slightly—she could feel it—but the snow muffled any noise.

In the morning, she had to brush aside nearly a foot of snow to find the trash the bear had left behind, and in the end she missed some of it; it would have to wait until the spring. In fact, she could hardly see any evidence that the bear had even been there. The ground was soft and white, and all its tracks were gone.

The winter settled in more deeply, and Claudia continued to train. She stuck with her Thursday-night classes, when the blueberry smell blanketed the town, but came for a few Mondays, too. Mostly she fenced the teenage boys, though she did face Evelyn when circumstances allowed it. Some classes, she spent a half-hour fencing herself, practising her lunge against one of the padded columns where Arthur had illustrated strike points on an opponent's torso with five small Xs made of white tape.

In the New Year, minutes before a class was to begin, Arthur took Claudia into his office and sat her in a chair before a desk.

"Wanted to show you something," he said. "I notice you sticking close to Evelyn, and I think that's great. She's exactly the kind of person you should be learning from."

Claudia had, before Christmas, indicated to Arthur a desire to test for her yellow armband—the next level up from the white beginner's stripe. Since then, Arthur had been speaking to her in terms of role models and good lessons and generally suggesting that she conceive of some sort of arc to her training and fencing goals.

Arthur shook a computer mouse, and the monitor on his right blinked on. He began clicking through folders. "Yup. Here." He turned the screen toward her.

Evelyn, in the photo, was beneath an opponent's strike, so low to the ground it was as though she'd found a hidden trough. Her left leg was splayed out straight behind her, the foot gently resting, instep to the ground. Her right leg was drawn up tight to her chest and planted so firmly it appeared to have roots. Her foil was in the shape of a comma, like it had corkscrewed through the air to find the tiny exposed spot on her opponent's flank. The photo was framed in such a way that you could see the scoring system lit up to record Evelyn's hit.

"Look at that," said Arthur. "This is what I want you to aspire to. The form. Look at the power. This is the payoff for her training. Look at the strength."

"Was this from before she hurt her knee?"

"She tell you about that?"

"Yeah."

"Yeah, probably not long before. She was ranked. She tell you that?"

"No."

"Didn't think so. She's not much of a self-promoter."

He faced the screen and stared silently for a moment, almost glassy-eyed. Feelings of leonine pride bumped visibly in his chest. "The form," he said, "the lower body. The lower body is magnificent here. Everything's where it should be."

"That's beautiful," agreed Claudia.

"That's it," he said. "Stick close to Evelyn. Do what she does. That'll teach you more than I can. That's all I wanted to say." He turned the monitor back toward himself and stared hard at the photo for another minute.

Claudia stood, left the office, and went across the dark floor to where she'd left her bag. She began preparing for class. Arthur asked her to lead the warm-up, and she felt no nerves. Only later did she consider what this meant: that she felt comfortable among them. She led them in the run, and the stretching up to the ceiling, and in pogo-hopping around the gym, the sweeps, and the wind sprints. She called out in the language in which she was gaining fluency, and all the bodies moved in response.

After a talk at the whiteboard on conditioning and on the fine points of the parry four, they left their foils on the floor and practised leaping into a lunge, starting at the end line and jumping forward as far as possible to land on one leg, the other held out behind them in a straight line. They balanced there, head raised to look forward, arms airplaned out to their sides, feeling their thighs burn and shake until Arthur released them. Then they did the other leg. Claudia anticipated, with some happiness, the warm ache she would feel in her legs as she lay alone in bed that night.

After that, they all picked up equipment and walked to pistes, to pair off and begin practice bouts. And just as

Claudia lowered her mask, preparing to fence a boy named Miles, Arthur called to her.

"Claudia, come get suited up to fence electric."

The only other fencer suited up for electronic scoring, with the silver lamé over her white jacket and breeches, was Evelyn.

Claudia understood that, at this point, winning wasn't the goal. Still, she felt a twinge of nerves. She held the younger woman with new regard now, with such reverence and esteem for who she'd been. *That photo*, Claudia thought, *was fucking marvellous.*

Evelyn helped her thread the body wire down the sleeve of her jacket, and then to slip on the lamé and plug it all in. They tested the scorer with their foils, and then they saluted and stood on guard.

We are martial and consecrated, Claudia thought, *engaged in this beautiful combat.*

They danced across the piste, feet thundering, their blades clanging with such lovely sounds.

Claudia scored an early point when Evelyn missed a heavy lunge and left herself vulnerable a beat too long. All Claudia had to do was poke Evelyn's chest, with as much effort as tacking up a photo with a pushpin. It surprised them both. Claudia could only just see Evelyn's eyes through their masks' screens, but she sensed anger in them. Anger not at Claudia, but at herself, for such a lapse. Failure to recover after a missed attack. Basic stuff, even Claudia knew. And she'd seen Evelyn fence enough to know that she was in for a barrage of attacks now. Evelyn didn't play it safe when she was cornered.

Evelyn kicked up her footwork, her blade movement. She came out of the en garde position in a flurry of metal.

Claudia decided she would do her best to weather it, and no more. She was still in awe. There would be no shame in being defeated by her hero.

Claudia listened to their footfalls, to the soft squeaking of the pulley wheels, to the buzzing of the scoring bible, and to Evelyn's soundings, grunts and sighs in response to her own efforts.

Evelyn tested Claudia's blade with a number of teasing taps, then struck quickly for the navel, but Claudia retracted her hips and flew her feet out backwards so that Evelyn's foil found only the empty air. Claudia tried a short, quick attack then, but was parried. The women traded offensive pushes, ping-ponging between the warning lines, but then Evelyn grew furious and Claudia could not even see her blade.

"Halt. Four-one," Arthur said, pointing at Evelyn. "*Prêt? Allez.*"

Evelyn flew at her again, and before the three-minute buzzer had time to sound, the score was nine to one.

Arthur called "Halt!" for the last time. Both women removed their masks, saluted, and stood with their shoulders heaving. That was all, for a moment. Just breathing. Then they moved toward one another and shook their left hands.

Evelyn smiled and said, "You're good, Claude, you did good."

Claudia, who'd now spent a year deciding her own truth, chose to believe her.

That night, Claudia found the bottom of a bottle of Cabernet Sauvignon. It was hellishly cold out, and the stars were hard and clear over the trees and the silver snow. She shovelled logs into the stove as the roof of her cabin popped and groaned. The fire was hot, maybe unsafely so, and she wore only a camisole and fleece leggings. She could feel the heat on her reddened arms and chest. The stereo throbbed with Taylor Swift.

Claudia lifted the iron poker from the stand next to the hearth. She held it halfway up its wooden handle, bent her legs, turned out her feet, and opened her hips until she was in the en garde position. She swung the tip of the heavy poker in a slow circle, pivoted until she was facing the oblong mirror on the wall over the walnut sideboard that had belonged to her mother's mother. *Look what you made me do, look what you just made me do*, she sang, parrying two imaginary advances. She shuffled backward and forward, then shot ahead in a lunge, the poker and her arm and her back leg forming a straight, upward line, the tip of her clumsy foil penetrating Smirnov's mask, piercing his eye.

There was the smallest sound, like a teacup being chipped by a spoon.

The glass at the centre of the mirror began to fault, and then to spiderweb out in delicate lines.

Claudia stood frozen—the poker still outflung, her sore legs still tensed, looking at the mirror's new blemish, unsure what to feel—until she decided that it was beautiful, and that she would leave it like that forever.

FORTUNATE PEOPLE

JILL AND T.E. TOOK ME IN when I was at my most dissolute. I was recently unemployed, and unemployable. All evidence suggested I was a losing proposition.

T.E. was on the history board at the university from which I'd been dismissed weeks earlier. He himself was not implicated, neither in canning me nor in the events which led to my canning. We were only colleagues with sympathetic characters. Yet T.E. still said: "We have a room, and we'd love to help you out if we can."

Wordless things can sometimes tell you all you need to know about a person. Shortly after he'd come aboard, when their first boy was just a few months old, he and Jill had me over for dinner. We all hit it off, and even then I knew I would like him. He must have sensed likewise. In T.E., I had found someone with a similar background to my own, and a comparable disdain for all of it, though he was better at concealing it than I.

In Jill I saw an easy acceptance, a personality questing for order and for contentedness with its surroundings— though with the earliest stirrings, I see now, of a resignation that these things might not come to pass. She was often happily weary, giving off the impression that her small family, and the chance to make things for them, were all she required to be happy.

Jill took photographs, very skilfully. Her camera was her eye; by watching her use it, you could come to understand what she valued. She trained the lens on T.E. in paternal moments, instances of tenderness toward the boys, of quiet interlocking. His large hand on Sam's back, Joshua's spindly arms around his father's summer-reddened neck. T.E. rarely appeared alone in Jill's photos. There was almost always a child.

She had deep Acadian roots and knew which seagrasses could be eaten, how they were to be cooked. She had alternate, more poetic-sounding names for everything that grew, crawled, or walked. Her French was effortless. She knew what to add to an empty white room to make it appear lived-in, comfortable. Her fingers were nimble and strong. She crocheted warm hats for her children, starting in summer and adding extra space to allow for their growth across the cooling months.

I remember her sitting in a folding chair beneath an apple tree while the boys splashed in a wading pool, and over it all the clouds pinned in place to a breathless sky. August, deep and hot. Jill's hair—not yet grey—tied up, off her neck.

There had been a series of women for me: rich, fragrant women, women with long legs, wide-brimmed hats. I was dazzled by them, the sureness with which they navigated the world in contrast with my own confoundedness, and I have been left haunted by the person I became in their presence.

Similarly, I looked at the way in which T.E. and Jill lived—at the life they had carved from stone, together— and failed to see how I could achieve anything similar. The wordless understanding, the silent division of roles, the co-operation, the fire still present in their limbs, the desire they never bothered to conceal. Yet they were still porous, they had not stopped allowing wonder to penetrate them. They gaped at the world alongside one another, energized by their boys' curiosity.

There was a daybed in a room Jill used for projects, crafts, for sitting. On the shelves, arranged sparely and tastefully, were photographs of Sam and Joshua, unframed, as well as European toys of wood and edgeless metal, puzzles, a bronze key gone mottled and dull, a pair of curved knitting needles, an old Jessi Colter LP. It was a neatly composed room, and though they offered it to me for as long as I might need, I knew that my presence—my duffle bag of clothing, and my shoes and belt and deodorant stick—tarnished it. I did my best not to spread myself out into that room, to keep my presence discreet. I failed at that, too.

T.E. had an analytic mind, a statistical bent, and was always organizing his thoughts on every given scenario. "It seems unlikely, given what I know," he told me, "that you'd try anything with Jill." It was a late-summer evening, warm and wet. Jill had gone to bed, leaving the two of us, a deck of cards, a bottle of wine, and the radio.

I assured him he was right, and he was. There is fair game, and there is the sacrosanct. I'm not too fallen to see the difference. At the very end of the evening I embraced him, heard his beard scratch against my collar, felt a warm tear on his cheek.

The boys were marvellous animals, creative, energetic. They laughed and screamed and played with such enthusiasm. The very precise and unique contours of their relationship were in place from an early age. They often communicated wordlessly, with gesture or a slight sound. They locked their arms around one another's necks and held whispered conferences.

I tried to be someone they would appreciate, a fun-uncle type, one in whom they could reveal something of themselves they wouldn't show their parents. I believe that children need such a presence in their lives. But I could never escape the feeling, when among them, that they maintained a wariness of my motives.

Only once, that I can remember, did their suspicion slip aside and allow something that felt like a genuine connection. I'd told Jill and T.E. that I wanted to repair the step on their back deck, which was suffering from rot so complete that the wood had gone soft and crumbly as bread. Sam was curious, and eager to help. He knew where the tools were kept in the old garage, so he went there and tried to lift the red metal box off the shelf. I came along after him and took the thing down, holding it by its handle while Sam held his arms over his head and placed his palms against the box's underside, trying to help take some of the weight of it.

Before I began, Sam wanted me to tell him what each tool was called and what it did, so we laid them all out on the deck's grey planks.

"That's a screwdriver, called a Phillips. See the end, a kind of plus sign?"

"Yeah," he said, examining it.

"Phillips. That's a claw hammer. Puts nails in and pulls them out, when you need it. That's a stud finder. Press the button." Nothing. "Must be out of batteries."

"What does it do?"

"It finds wood where you can't see it."

Using scrap wood from other projects, I restored the step. I also vowed to apply fresh stain to it and to the rest of the deck as well, to forestall further rot, and to make it less splintery beneath the boys' bare feet. I never got around to it. The step, I'm certain, is still bare wood, and the rest of the deck cries out for a new coat, going to dust and paper, closer each day to collapse. But I had intended to do it, with all sincerity. And then the holidays came, and snow.

I was an awkward addition to their family Christmas, but they were so gracious that it hurts me to think about it now.

At New Year's, there was a party which T.E. and Jill insisted I attend with them, thrown by neighbourhood friends, no children. They'd hired a girl from across the street to sit the boys, fourteen, very responsible.

"You'll have a great time," said T.E. "Very nice people. And wonderful food."

"I'm dressing up," said Jill. "I never do. You don't want to miss it."

I had a shirt, black pants. T.E. lent me a coat and a tie. I felt unnatural in them, but my friends insisted I looked nice. I'm still not able to determine whether I actually did, though I have seen photos. I'm still inside my own head, feeling what I felt then.

I wondered that night, and have wondered since, if their motivation was to find me a new love. There were several women there, single, a few single mothers, and one woman whose marriage was clearly hanging by its last threads and who seemed open to being led away. Women in their thirties, with intelligence and amassed wisdom, good boots, clear eyes. They were all lovely and comfortable, easy conversationalists, distracted but seemingly sincere. I thought about falling in love that evening, but decided against it. It was easier to drift among those people, smile at their remarks, eat their food, without worrying about what they'd think of me in the future.

T.E. was hunched, uneasy, stand-offish. It makes sense when I look back on it now, but I really had no idea then. I was as ignorant to what was going on as Jill was. When midnight came, I watched Jill throw her arms around his neck and kiss his cheek, but he did not look at her. He seemed to be looking out the window, toward something I could not see: a future, I now think, which looked nothing like the life he knew.

Jill looked fresh and happy. Younger than she ever had, for as long as I'd known her. That said, I don't know that I ever found Jill beautiful. It was beside the point, I saw from the beginning. A love would hang between us, but one that romantic or sexual feelings would have only profaned. Those were not our roles.

She was so steady and measured through all of it. It was heartbreaking and admirable. It taught me something about how one should carry oneself when the chips are down.

Only once did she ever show me anything raw, something she couldn't contain. An animal intensity. It lasted only for the briefest of moments, and then it was gone. It was a breath, a blink.

It was a year after their dissolution. She had rented a house in Tadoussac for the month of July so that she and the boys could find themselves somewhere quite different to make memories of this new life of theirs, the life without T.E. Jill said I should come visit for a weekend, so I made the drive from Montreal and ended up staying six nights, sleeping on a cot in a turret atop the strange house, windows on all sides, reached through a trap door and a ladder down to the second floor.

One breezy afternoon, we walked on the rocks where the St. Lawrence meets the Saguenay. The footing was slippery, the water cold. Jill and I sat in the sun, watching the water glint, a freighter in the distance on its slow path west. The boys were hurling pebbles into the river. They had been warned to watch themselves, to show caution on the wet rocks, but Sam slipped anyway, disappearing from sight before popping back up, his hair wet. He stood in water up to his armpits and called for his mother, screaming in terror, though the danger appeared minor. It was possible he might slip from where he was standing and go under again, but as long as he stayed still he would be fine. And yet the fear on his face was something awful.

Jill said, only, "Oh God, Sam, hold on."

By then I was on my feet and racing toward the shore. Slowing as I neared, I made to crouch so that I could pull him up, but my feet went out just as Sam's had, and I wound up in the water standing next to the boy. I very quickly lifted him under his arms and placed him on a dry spot of rock. His mother reached him a moment later and threw her arms around him.

I expect I seemed a bit ridiculous standing there in that cold, shallow water, but then Jill fixed me with a look that was the most ferocious and inflamed that I had ever seen on her. Her skin was flushed and her lips shockingly red. There was something undeniably fierce in her just then, and I wondered later if she hadn't seen me differently in that moment, too. But by the time I was out and drying myself on the sunny rocks, it was gone, and nothing between us was different. For that I remain grateful.

We walked back along a rocky trail and down to the wharf, me feeling quite humiliated, my shorts and shoes and shirt soaked and clinging to my body. Sam was wet, too, of course, but was perfectly happy. It's terrible to think that I might have felt better had he seemed more affected, more upset, but I believe that might have been the case.

At the place where the beach stands below Tadoussac, just before the grand old hotel, we made to cross the road.

A woman driving a small motorized scooter stopped to let us by. Behind her, a man in a green pickup truck, unaware of us, swung wide around the scooter and continued on.

Sam and Joshua were walking just in front of me and did not see the truck coming around, so I put my hands on their shoulders to stop them in their tracks. As the pickup passed, I raised my hands in a gesture to the driver. He must still not have seen the boys, because he smiled warmly and waved back at me.

PIGEON

I WAS THE MIDDLE of three children.

The eldest of us, our sister Charlotte, was living with our aunt in Toronto. Just sixteen, she was already working in a coffee shop, determined—she had told us—to put our branch of the family squarely behind her. Charlotte taught herself guitar, and later travelled to Vancouver and eventually Los Angeles with a band for which she sang and wrote songs. Whether they're still together and making music, and where she or they might be, I can't now say with any authority. Someone told me she'd had a daughter, but I don't know for certain.

With our mother gone from our lives, that left me with Gavin—three years my junior—and our father, Caspar Milledge.

That first summer, after we'd been out of school a week, Dad rented a little wooden cottage for a week at Six Foot Bay Resort. He was thirty-eight years old then. His hair had not yet begun to thin—it was thick and dark brown, and he wore it a little bit long, swept to one side. He had a pushbroom moustache and a perpetual stubble on the rest of his face, though he shaved often and usually smelled faintly of Brut aftershave. He was of average height and naturally thin, but with the ambient doughiness of a man who gets little exercise and who is drunk more nights than he isn't. He appeared, I know, normal for those times, in that place.

We drove up to the resort in his battered Oldsmobile, listening to the one and only cassette he kept in the car: an album of Cure remixes. Skittery, echoing noises bounced between the speakers, and Robert Smith sang from the bottom of a well. Our familiarity with that tape did nothing to rob it of its strangeness, which increased as the sound gradually degraded, the layers slowly stripped off the magnetic tape by wear, time, and oxygen, the music becoming incrementally more hollow-sounding and alien. It was not the sort of music my father generally listened to, but someone had given him the tape, and he listened to it endlessly— trying, I think, to understand it. He wasn't a person who listened to music for pleasure. Songs, for him, were a kind of puzzle, a riddle, as though by solving them he would learn what made other people happy. Years later, Gavin would suggest that he might have been trying to find our mother.

Dad said on the drive up that he was going to teach us to fish, though I had never known him to do it, and though neither Gavin nor I had ever expressed the faintest interest in it. Two days into our week there we hadn't put a single hook in the water. The whole first day we didn't even leave the cottage; he sat in a deck chair, read magazines, and drank beer, while Gavin and I passed the same half-dozen comic books back and forth.

Early on the morning of the second day, our father woke us excitedly.

"You've gotta see this!" he shouted, so we followed him outside. Parked out front was a four-wheeled off-road golf cart. "I rented it for the day."

Gavin was clearly excited. I pretended to be, but in truth I harboured a fear of anything motorized. When I was much younger I'd had some kind of premonition that I'd one day lose a limb, or possibly even my life, to such a thing. I don't know why, exactly, but I've never totally shaken the thought.

After we had Corn Pops and big glasses of Sunny Delight

in the cabin's tiny kitchenette, we started out. A strong, hot wind riffled the lake and the trees over our heads. It was early in the morning but the heat was already enough to make you think twice about moving. Our sweaty thighs stuck to the cart's vinyl seats.

Dad lurched the vehicle forward, had it stall, and then restarted it, before moving us along more smoothly across the resort's broad lawn and up the gravel road which led into it. We began the first half of the day, as the heat grew caustic and the air stiller and stiller, slowly navigating the back roads of cottage country, piloting the very loud cart along snowmobile trails, fire routes, and gravel access roads. We stopped at rocky outcrops overlooking coves and inlets, and at the heads of trails which snaked down through cottagers' properties toward the lake.

Our father was looking for a specific rock that he and his late brother Bert had discovered as boys. He'd told us about it before. It was, he said, the perfect spot to jump into Pigeon Lake: a fifteen- or twenty-foot drop into bottomless blackness. They did all manner of dives, cannonballs, and backflips. Even swam from there to Fothergill Island, which was rimmed with beach and criss-crossed by trails. He told us it was a place perfect for adventure—that the summer their parents rented a cabin for a whole month was the greatest summer of his life.

He was lost in his search for this spot. Much of the time, he seemed to forget Gavin and I were even there. Other times, he muttered to us about trees or bends in gravel roads that he was adamant he recognized. "Yes! It's right around here. That tree looks familiar. We're close, boys." Each time he was wrong, but every error only fuelled him with a new desperation to find the right place. So we'd climb back into the cart, Gavin on my lap in the passenger seat, and our father would fire the thing back to life, and we'd rumble off to the next site.

I was beginning to suspect that we weren't even on Pigeon Lake. It seemed likely to me that we were still on Sandy Lake, site of our rented cottage, two lakes over from Pigeon. I shared this with Gavin when our father had wandered thirty feet away from us to inspect a small hill, and Gavin thought I might be right.

But because he was our father, we tried to believe in him. We tried to imagine a world in which his belief was enough to overcome simple facts. We were not yet old enough to allow our impatience and our experience to shape our thoughts in defiance of him. We were, then, still his.

So we drove. He steered us over rutted gravel roads lined in oak and white pine, beaver-sawn stumps, trillium patches, and low wetlands. The cart's engine was loud and shook violently. Everything he saw sparked a memory in him, but the place he was so desperate to find remained out of reach.

Our father drove the cart one-handed. In his free hand he kept a plastic coffee cup, holding something other than coffee. That was normal for him. I don't remember just how old I was when he taught me that it was possible to fit an entire bottle of beer in a coffee mug, but I'm certain I was too young for such knowledge. As he drove, he kept telling us about his brother. "Bertie tried to teach himself to swan dive. Come out black and blue every time," he'd say over the roar of the motor, then take another swig. "Never failed."

Later, we would come to recognize this as the point at which my father's lifelong alcoholism had begun to bleed into the soft, porous edge of the dementia which would characterize the last third of his life. It was the beginning of our slow-motion loss.

Dad had always been different. Even we could tell he was, sequestered as we were within the life that he—and, at least initially, our mother—had built, or perhaps cordoned off for us from the rest of the world. We knew how a normal father might behave, by observation and by the stories that filtered to us through friends, and when we turned to look back at our own family with that knowledge, we understood that Caspar Milledge was not a normal father.

The reason is clear in retrospect: his unpredictability. Early on, that unpredictability meant ice cream for dinner, and maybe for breakfast the next morning, too. It meant skipping school to drive to Toronto to go up the CN Tower because the clouds that morning were beautiful and our father wanted us to see what they might look like from a thousand feet above the ground. Such episodes were common, and they were thrilling. But as we got older, Dad's unpredictability meant missing soccer practice. Or living eighteen months without kitchen counters because he'd decided they needed replacing, had spent a Saturday afternoon tearing them out, and then—either through lack of funds or losing focus—never gotten around to putting anything else in their place.

Over the course of our lives to that point—I was eleven, Gavin was eight—we had come to a place of familiarity with him, despite being unable to predict his actions. We were not surprised when he did something surprising.

I don't know how that set us up for the rest of our lives. Families fracture. It happens all the time, and as often as not, those caught up in such events recover and resume their life's path. They do just fine. We've all seen that. Who's to say what caused Gavin's later addictions, his inability to sustain a relationship, his frequent and varied dealings with the law? Whether that was the result of our father's actions, I can't say. I wouldn't care to make that call.

We hunted in vain all morning, yet my father's only regret was that his cup grew empty. It was only when he openly debated going back to the cabin to resupply that I think he realized he'd either forgotten how far we'd come, or just how to get back there. It wasn't embarrassment I saw on his face then, but utter bewilderment. "If I could just," I heard him say to himself, and then nothing else.

He was starting to leave a lot of sentences unfinished then.

When Gavin complained of hunger, our father reacted as if seized by a great idea. "Oh," he said, and stopped the cart. He put one foot out the door, stood, stuffed both hands in his shorts pockets, and pulled out a granola bar in each fist. He seemed both shocked and pleased by his forethought, and I realized what had struck him a moment earlier was the memory of having planned ahead—something rare enough to be notable.

Satisfied that he'd carried out a parental duty, he stepped back into the cart and we roared off down another dirt road. "We're on an adventure," he kept saying, as if to head off any complaints out of us.

Then, suddenly, we stopped. I think Gavin was dozing, or at least drifting away from our immediate surroundings, because when Dad mashed the brakes, Gavin was nearly ejected over the little dash. He fell off my lap and thudded to the floor of the cart. Our father failed to notice. I helped Gavin out of the tight space at my feet, put my arms around him, and apologized for not catching him.

We were at a place where the road—or cart path, really—came around a bend and then narrowed, before terminating beneath a canopy of very old pine and spruce trees. It was a road meant to service the two or three properties on a point extending into a lake, which our father believed was Pigeon.

Dad was on his feet before the buggy came to a complete stop, and rushed into the forested ditch next to the road. In the direction my father was headed was a cabin, a small, square shack with a dark shingled roof and grey-brown cedar siding. A car was parked next to it. Beyond it, through the trees, was the lake, shimmering and spectral, just out of reach. Between us and all of that—the cabin, the car, the lake—was a bare rock surrounded by coniferous trees and a low tangle of thorny weeds and berry bushes. It glared baldly and flatly beneath the hot sun. Dad stood at the edge of it.

There was a woman. She must have been there all along, but I only noticed her once Gavin quit gasping for breath. We'd stood up, both of us, and had come around the front of the cart with the intention, I suppose, of following Dad.

"Hello," she said, with a hint of question, a non-aggressive challenge. She had come from behind the car, I think, probably after hearing the cart's obnoxious engine getting closer and closer. She was maybe forty, sandy-haired, with a long ponytail, wearing a grey tank top and olive canvas shorts, a pair of white Keds on her feet. She began walking toward Dad, but when he looked up at her she stopped.

I couldn't see Dad's face from where I was standing, but I know the expression he must have been wearing: crazed, nearly, or fixed, his eyes big and his mouth a determined straight line below his moustache. It was a look I knew my father to take on unconsciously, when someone tried, unsuccessfully, to commandeer his attention while he was focused on something else. Usually it was me or Gavin, and we were almost always out of luck.

"Can I help you," the woman said. This time there was a high ring overtop her voice, a tension like a guy wire in a high wind.

Our father stirred as if woken. "Hi. Okay," he said. "Sorry. These are my sons, and this is a spot where I came. We swam. My brother and I."

"How nice," she said, with some suspicion.

"We were kids. Their age," he said, looking at us. "I was hoping to bring them here so they could swim, too."

"It's a good spot," she said, "but when did you do that?"

"Oh, a long time ago."

"Okay," she said. "Are you sure this is the place where you did that? This is my family's place. All this. Always was." She crossed her arms across her chest and held her shoulders.

"Must have been before the place was built," he said. "I remember this rock, and the way the bay dips in here. Exactly like I remember it."

"Sorry, I really think you have the wrong place," she said. "The cottage is almost fifty years old. You really don't look old enough to have come here before it was built."

"Oh, I think you're wrong," he said.

It's hard now for me to describe just how unremarkable the spot we were standing in was, for that part of the world. We could have been next to any one of a thousand lakes in the area. There were trees, and rocks, exposed roots, and the tiniest wind coming gently off a picturesque lake, all of it beneath a hot summer sun, staring back at us with a stony indifference. There were many structures like the woman's cottage, some of them decades old but still appearing temporary, destined to fade and be forgotten, while all the rest of it persisted. I doubted, taking all of this in, that my father truly believed what he was saying to the woman.

"Please," she said, now appearing a little agitated. "I'm sorry, but this isn't the place you remember."

"Pigeon Lake," he shouted. "I just want to take my boys swimming in Pigeon goddamn Lake!"

Gavin backed into me, visibly afraid, aware even at his age that our father could always be counted on to say the wrong thing, angering or confusing or tainting strangers, convincing them of our recklessness and strangeness by association.

"I'm sorry," she said. "See? This is Sandy Lake."

"No," he said too quickly, "no. Nice try."

"Sir," she said, "please, I'm sorry to say, but you and your sons are on the wrong lake. If you go back out the road until—"

"No, that's wrong," he said through clenched teeth, a bit of colour coming to the back of his neck. "You're wrong and I know it. Sorry, miss. Sorry. But I'd like to show them myself."

He leaned forward and took a step. Though she stood twenty paces away, she took a step back.

"No, please," she said, determined but obviously unconvinced of her ability to make him see the sense in what she was saying. "I have to ask you to leave."

"Are you kidding me," our father said. "Are you goddamn well kidding me?" He stopped walking and looked at her with something like astonished anger or, if I'm to extend my father any charity, honest incredulity—incredulity, perhaps at the ease with which loss sneaks up on and then overtakes us. "You really mean to tell me that this isn't the place I remember?"

"No. I'm sorry."

"Well, Jesus, I can't believe this. You've got nerve."

"I'm sorry?"

"Lying like that. I get it. You look at me and you don't trust me. But okay, look at these boys. Do they look like scam artists?"

"I'm sure you're not trying anything, sir," she said, "but you really do have to go."

"Put up a sign or something. *Private Property: Keep Off.* Get a gun and you can wave it at people like me who just want to see the lake. I think that's pretty awful, ma'am."

"Please."

"With all due," he said, and stopped. He knotted up and held his breath in his chest for a moment.

She had taken a few more steps back, toward her car. I didn't blame her. I knew what it looked like when he was kept from something he'd set his mind on. It looked ugly. He intended only to resurrect a memory, to splash in the water of his boyhood—but she had no way of knowing that. I know he would not have harmed her, but I also knew, even then, the threat a man posed to a woman, knew that she had to remain wary for her own protection. The fear in her eyes was palpable, and it left in me such an overwhelming state of helplessness. I couldn't communicate with her any more than I could with my father. We were all, in that tableau, completely isolated from one another.

Finally, he moved. Dad came back to the road, kicked some gravel off into the weeds and scrub, then sat down heavily on the cart's seat. His face was red.

"Get in, guys, and we'll head back," he said to us quietly.

He started the buggy and continued a few yards down the road until we reached its end, then piloted the cart through a tight one-hundred-and-eighty-degree arc to retrace our route back past the woman's cabin.

She was still standing on the other side of her car, watching us, her hands near her throat.

We kept driving back up the road for ten or fifteen minutes. When we reached a point where the road branched, our father stopped and got out and began pacing. "Fucking hell," he said. He looked at me, I suppose because I was the oldest child there, and he said, confidingly, "It's a hell of a thing. This age. Too old to be stupid, too young to be wise."

He looked suddenly at the forest then, as though a voice from there had spoken to him.

"Why don't you care?" he asked.

At first I thought he was talking to Gavin and me. But he wasn't, he was directing his question to a tree, or the trees, or to everything he saw, all the wild and untamed things before him, the things to which our lives did not matter at all, not our thoughts or our achievements.

We remained lost until nearly sundown, and when we finally found the resort again, my father said nothing about Pigeon Lake, or swimming with his brother, or any of it.

The rest of the week, we spent all our time reading and sleeping and not fishing. Counting the hours until we could leave the Six Foot Bay Resort and go back to our messy home life with our sick father and our missing mother and our absent sister and no countertops and the faulty set of expectations with which we'd been equipped. Back to life as we knew it.

What aches most in me now, when I think of that episode, is the complete and utter uselessness of love and all its attendant emotions in the face of such intractable things as loss and decay. My hopefulness and affection could not bring our father back from the dark forest into which he was receding. His love for us—which I know he felt, for all his missteps and lapses—was a leash he had dropped and then watched slip away through the uncut grass. It would do him no good. Everything I remember of him is, in one form or another, a vision of us losing him, and him losing us. The process, worming into his memories and his logic centres, was likely underway before we were even born, and would not halt. Though he would live another twenty years, he would become a man we could not recognize, and who would not know us in turn. Not our faces, not even our names.

BROADCASTING

WHEN WE LIVED in Yuma, I had the great sense of being on the edge of things. I felt that if I stood with my back to the east, all of civilization—all of our history, all our losses and debts—would be behind me. Though of course that was not true.

After my radio job in Ottawa disappeared, the way they often do, I had to take the first thing I could find. I ended up producing for a low-wattage oldies station in Watertown, New York. It was a mostly disagreeable little place that I nonetheless managed, mostly through an exercise of will, to find charming in pockets. The house I had us living in was right next to a playground, which my daughter Candace, who was around three then, loved. I found a teenage girl named Jennifer—the cheery daughter of the woman who answered phones at the station—to babysit for me. There was a nice enough bar nearby, Milton's. And sometimes, when I drove around town or walked home from the bar, I would catch a glimpse of the river, or the void in the night where I knew the river was, and I'd even find myself thinking that Watertown was pretty.

Shona would join me there most weekends. We had worked together at a station in Ottawa, back when radio jobs were more plentiful. Before automation, before centralization. She'd been married to an ad salesman there, or attached anyway, but things didn't work out, and she and I became close in the aftermath. Eventually she'd tired of being a radio journalist, so she got her certification as a yoga instructor and had been doing that for a few years by the time I moved to Watertown. She said it was a thing that travelled well, because anywhere you were likely to find yourself, you'd find people who were overtired and stressed and needed what yoga offered. *Grounding*, she said.

She was still in Ottawa, but could do the drive in under two hours. Apparently, she found that an acceptable price to pay for my company. "I like driving," she'd say. "Gives me time to spend with myself."

When she'd come, generally on a Friday, I'd get Jennifer to watch Candace so that Shona and I could be grown-ups and go to dinner. Usually, we'd wind up at Milton's. One thing I admired about Shona was the fact that her dedication to wellness and groundedness did not interfere with her great thirst. It meant that we could have a few rounds, careen home, put Jennifer in a cab, and afterwards still open up a bottle of something hard before falling onto the bed.

On nights like those, inevitably, we'd talk about the future. We avoided doing so in the sober daylight hours—it was an unspoken policy of ours—but on those nights, things loosened up, and we became free dreamers, big planners, lovers of a grand tomorrow.

"What if we'd met ten years earlier?" she asked me once.

"You wouldn't have liked me then," I said.

"I didn't really like Dan either, but I stuck with him. I could have been Candace's mom."

"Oh, who knows. Would you have wanted that?" I asked, and looked over at the silhouette of her face against the light leaking in under the bedroom door. I had put a night-light in the hallway for Candace, who sometimes got up and wandered around in the dark.

"Your baby? Your babies? I think so."

"You'd be a good mom. Candace is crazy about you."

"So's her dad," she said, and flipped herself over on top of me, laughing.

Candace was always a sound sleeper, so Shona and me, we'd have ourselves a party until we couldn't sustain it any longer, and then we'd give in to sleep, or something deeper. Hours later, with the dim, dirty light of a Watertown morning peeking around the curtains, we'd wake up and have to make some sense of Saturday morning. And then on Saturday night we'd do it all again.

It was costing me something near a fortune. Every visit meant two dinners plus drinks, and two nights of babysitting. It was exhausting, too. But I loved it and wouldn't have dreamed of going without it.

Overall, though, I felt a bit like I was spinning my wheels in Watertown. The summer was fine and warm, and while there wasn't much to do, it was a pleasant enough place to do nothing. But as it got colder, I could feel something clamping down on us: a tightness, a way of life that was small and too contained.

I began thinking that as long as I was working in the States, we might as well find somewhere nicer to be, or warmer anyway. Maybe California.

While scouring an online job board, I came across the opening in Yuma. It wasn't California, but the Arizona desert seemed close enough. It seemed to possess an edge, a frontier feeling. I needed that. In Watertown, there were no edges—just the slow, slumping shape of your life going flat in the middle. Not horribly, and perhaps not even all that sadly. But eventually I think you wake up in a place like Watertown and say to yourself, *Why didn't I go to Yuma?* And all the answers you could come up with would feel pretty unsatisfactory.

"What do you think of Yuma?" I asked Shona one wild night in November, as we lay all twisted together in that cold bed.

"I think of Gary Cooper," Shona said.

"You're thinking of *High Noon*," I said. "Somebody else was in *3:10 to Yuma*."

"Then they remade it with what's his name."

"The Australian guy."

"Crowe," she said. "Russell Crowe."

"Right. And Batman. Christian Bale."

"Why do you want to know about Yuma?" she asked.

"I'm thinking of going there. Moving there."

"Sure you are."

"No, I mean it. There's an opening at a station there, and I'm sick of this cold. And winter hasn't even hit yet."

"What do I think," she said, narrowing her eyes and pushing her lips out into a pout. "I think you can't just keep jumping around, Russ, is what I think. Candace needs a home."

"Maybe, sure, yes," I said. "But what I figure is I find her one now, before she starts school. Kids her age, they adapt. They're very good at it."

Shona got up then and stretched her arms above her head. I could just make her out in the dark, wearing nothing but her black underwear. She walked across the room and opened the door, went into the bathroom. I closed my eyes and listened to my own breathing and the whine of the pipes as she ran water.

When she came back, she sat on the side of the bed near

me and she put her hand on my chest. "I can't tell if you're serious," she said.

"I am. Why wouldn't I be?"

"And you're asking me to come?"

"Yes. I expect people do yoga in Yuma, too."

"Of course they do."

"So?"

I know that Shona, at that point in her life, was feeling a lot like I was: without vista, without a chance to see things. Hemmed in by a lot of small stuff. I didn't think then that it was cowardly to drop your life and take up a new one, in a new place, so long as you weren't hurting anyone. I couldn't see what might be holding me and Candace to Watertown, or Shona to Ottawa. Yes, everything was fine enough—but why couldn't it be even better?

I thought we owed it to ourselves to try.

"Give me time, Russ. I need to think about this. To figure out what's best for me."

"I understand," I said, though I didn't. Not then.

We got up the next morning to find that the snow had begun. The sense I had then, that the winter would not end until April or May, sealed things for me, though I did not and would not say that to Shona.

The snow was still flying when she left us on Sunday afternoon, and the roads looked awful. I bundled Candace up in her snowsuit and we went out in our small driveway to dig out Shona's car. Shona had only a pair of high-heeled boots with her, and wore a small leather coat with one of her big, luxurious scarves elaborately wrapped around her neck and shoulders. She looked lovely, though cold, and I had to be aware of the chance that I wouldn't see her again.

"You don't have snows on this car," I said.

"All-seasons. They're good. I'm good."

"All-seasons aren't for all seasons. It's a bad name. I need you to get home safe, Shon," I said. "I need you to go easy and take your time."

"Yes, baby," she said, in a way that was sweet, but also, I knew, making a little fun of me, of the parental me, the worrier, the protector.

"Can you let me know when you get there?" I said. "Call or text?"

I put my hands on her face then, and I thought about those invisible signals, the ones that carry words, carry sounds, pass through our clothing and bodies, through walls and features of the landscape.

"I will," she said, and nodded, then kissed me. She stooped, kissed and hugged Candace, who'd been standing by my feet, and then she stood and kissed me again, harder, more desperately, like a person who is starving. After that, she climbed into her car, and was gone.

The long and short of it is that I gave my notice and gathered our few things, and by the New Year we were in Yuma, my little girl and I.

The drive gave us the chance to see the Grand Canyon. Candace didn't quite seem to believe it was real—as though it were a thing I'd dreamed up and shown her, and after we turned our backs it would dissolve. I held her in my arms and we stood near the lip of it, the ground falling away from us, the sky set to swallow us. Everything wild.

I told her, "For now you'll have to take my word for it, but that's one of the most amazing things you'll ever see."

"It's pretty," she said—fearing, I could tell, that my feelings would be hurt if she did not praise the sight. She is, at times, as sensitive as her mother was.

Of the desert she said, over and over again, "Where's the trees?"

"In this part of the world, they're cactuses. But you don't say cactuses, you say cacti."

"Prickles!"

When we got to Yuma, I took a little suite in a motel among the RV parks and minigolf courses on the edge of town. Candace had her side of the room and I had mine, a counter and a lattice divider running half the length of the room in between. I sat on the bed and watched college football while running my hands over the keyboard of a laptop, looking for a place for us to rent.

Before we'd left, I'd been in touch with the manager of STAR 100.9, who'd been kind of non-committal about her desire to meet with me. "I'm coming to Yuma anyway," I'd said on the phone, "so I'd appreciate a chance to sit down and tell you why I'm right for your station."

"Why don't you get in touch when you arrive here?" she'd said.

I got the uneasy sense that there was no longer an opening, or at least not an opening for me. But I bullied ahead anyway, thinking my enthusiasm might translate into good things for Candace and me.

It only took a few days to find a house. It was a two-bedroom place with a kitchen the size of a closet and a scrubby little yard. Dogs roamed freely and howled all night and the Interstate zoomed past my bedroom window. I put down first and last rent, and started to furnish it with finds from the Goodwill. After a couple of nights on the floor I found a futon for Candace, and for me an old oak bed frame, thick and dramatic, into which I dropped a Craigslist mattress. Life rolled on.

The station manager—her name was Wendy Farquhar—continued to deflect, and I figured I'd better find something temporary in case this radio business took too long in coming together. I presented myself at the jobs office downtown, gave them my old road-construction credentials, and found myself on a crew a few days later. Meanwhile, Candace was being watched by a mom in the neighbourhood, a woman named Felicia, who had two of her own and another in her care. Paying her, plus the rent, plus the new furniture and things, on top of the gas and food and motels for the trip down, had me scratching the bottom of the barrel and needing that first road-crew cheque pretty badly.

The heat was like nothing else. I can't describe it to you. I lost ten pounds my first week with the crew. We were on a stretch of I-8 to the east of the city, just over the hills, where agricultural land hugged the river on the one side, and the other was pure, parched Sonoran waste. I stood all day in that godless sun with a shovel in my hand, or a rake, bent over steaming asphalt, or holding a flag. My skin baked and my feet roasted in my old steel-toes.

At the end of the day, I'd drive under the limit and take in the sight of the light dyeing everything pink and blue, the rock and the sand, the fields of citrus. I'd park at the house and find Candace playing with the other children in a yard nearby while Felicia sat watching and chatting in Spanish with another woman, who may have been her sister. I'd fetch Candace, and if anything bad had happened that day, Felicia would tell me, but usually I'd just wave and she'd smile and wave, too. Then Candace and

I would go inside, and I'd get her some juice and open myself a beer. I'd have a quick shower. We'd debate what to have for dinner but usually just open a can of spaghetti, then watch some TV together. At bedtime we'd read a book or two, then she'd lie in the dark and talk to her unicorn awhile before drifting off, whereupon I would watch some more TV, and maybe chat with Shona on the phone. And that was life. It wasn't a bad one.

A seam of sadness still ran through it, though.

I rattled around feeling like I was waiting for the last piece to fall into place. At first I assumed that last piece was the radio job, but as the days passed I was more and more certain that I wasn't going to find myself in the employ of STAR 100.9. That disappointed me, but it didn't tarnish things so completely. The truth was, I didn't mind working the roads. What was actually missing, of course, was Shona's company.

The feeling was made harder by our telephone calls. Her voice soothed me, but it also made me desperate for her skin, her smell, her eyes. I wanted to feel her presence, not just to know how she was getting on in Ottawa.

"Shon, is this enough for you?" I asked her one night.

"It's what we have."

"You remember what I asked you?"

"I'm not forgetting it. I know the invitation's open."

"It is. It is open. I hope you'll think about it some more."

"I could hardly think about it more, babe."

"But no decision yet."

"It's a complicated thing, isn't it?"

"I suppose it is."

I got high one night with my new neighbours, Joe and Mercedes. They lived two doors down, in a little house with an enormous cactus out front. I'd see them around a lot because Joe was a programmer who worked from home and Mercedes was home-schooling their two, Annabel and Sonny. Annabel and Candace sometimes played together, which was how I got to talking with Joe.

Joe said I ought to come over for a drink one night, so I did. I put Candace down to sleep and cracked her window and then slipped out. When I got to their house, Joe and Mercedes were on their front step, drinking wine and laughing. "The Canadian!" Joe said.

I had the sense pretty quickly that he was the kind to watch you eat an apple and then tell you that you were doing it wrong because you didn't eat the core. I wasn't far off—but he was all right. Kind of funny about his cynicism. He made me laugh.

"Good evening, Joe," I said.

He introduced me to Mercedes, who I'd seen around but hadn't yet spoken to. She was dark-haired and her face was lined and her cool, green eyes were sad but not unfriendly. Mercedes, I'd learn, was the optimistic one, the one who'd invite their kids to paint giant sunshines on their bedroom walls and then smile at the messy results.

She said, "Is your little one sleeping?"

I said yes, and pointed to the glow of her nightlight in the window.

"She's a sweet little girl," Mercedes said.

"Thank you," I said. "She's everything to me."

They both smiled at this, and were silent. I felt that they were thinking of their children, of how important Sonny and Annabel were to their lives.

"Yours are asleep?" I asked.

"I think so," Mercedes said. "They were tired. We don't enforce a bedtime. We let them decide when they're ready for bed. We find that way they don't resent it. It's not a bad thing. It's what they want."

"We believe in self-direction," said Joe.

"And it works? I just imagine my girl would try to stay up all night."

"She'd get used to it," Joe said, smiling.

I nodded and tried to seem open to such ideas, but thought to myself that it wasn't a thing I'd ever do. Maybe it was common sense, or maybe it was an old, rusty idea to which I was welded, but I thought kids needed a bedtime. I still do.

Something about Mercedes and Joe backed up this idea I'd had about Yuma being on the edge of things. They were experimenting with everything. They felt like old rules didn't apply to them. It inspired in me a mix of envy and pity that I would never have expressed to them.

"You need a drink," Joe said. "What can we get you? Beer? Wine? Something more exotic?"

"I'd take a beer, Joe," I said.

He nodded and bounded up the steps and into the house, letting the screen door slap behind him.

"Tell me something about Canada," Mercedes said. "We've never been."

"There are a lot more trees than there are here," I said, and smiled.

"And snow?"

"In winter. Where I'm from, the winters are long and hard. Lots of snow."

"I guess you just get used to it," she said. "I can't imagine it."

"It's just life there," I said. "It can be fun."

Joe banged back out the door and handed me a bottle I didn't recognize. "Drink local," he said.

I don't think Joe was yet forty, but he had some miles on him. His bushy, greying hair stuck out from beneath a weathered tweed flat cap, his quick brown eyes set deep in his lined, tanned face. He had a grey goatee that drew attention to his mouth, which always looked on the verge of saying something.

The night seemed very dark then, though warm and soft. We huddled beneath the lamp on the front step of their small home and talked about our children because it was something we had in common.

"I hope you won't mind me asking," Mercedes said, "but where is Candace's mother?"

"That's a story," I said. "Well, she had some trouble soon after Candace was born, and we couldn't find any way to help her. She went away for a while and then tried to come back, but it wasn't any good. And our families agreed, you know, that it would be best if I took care of Candace. And a judge agreed that that was true."

"Oh, Russ, I'm sorry I asked."

"Don't be sorry. It's what happened. I'm not ashamed of it. I don't know where she is now, but I hope she's better. I hope we did the right thing for her."

Things were quiet for a few moments after that. Finally Joe broke the silence to talk about computers. Mercedes asked if there was anyone new in my life. "I think so," I said.

Joe got me another beer. Then he said, "Do you mind if we smoke, Russ?" I said no, of course I didn't mind, so he took a small tin and a pack of papers from the pocket of his New York Yankees sweatshirt and rolled quickly and expertly. He was an artist, a practised one. He looked me in the eyes while his fingers worked mechanically, producing the smoothest, tightest joint I had ever seen.

Mercedes asked if I ever got high.

"I have no policy against it," I said.

So we passed the thing around while we sat quietly, listening to the dogs bark and to the cars whoosh by on the highway. The night had had a pretty, sweet scent to it, but that was pushed aside by the strong smell of our smoking.

Joe held the fumes for a long time, then let them slowly out, and laughed. Mercedes giggled.

"Our small reward," he said.

"There isn't much left to us, is there?"

"Are you happy, Russ?" Mercedes asked.

"I don't know. I'm getting close, maybe," I said. "I believe it's possible to be happy. That marks a bit of a change for me."

"Good for you," she said, and leaned forward to pat my arm, then handed me the joint.

"I have something else for us," Joe said. "Just give me a few minutes."

"Okay," I said. "What the hell." It was getting late, but I was enjoying myself. I'd feel it the next day, but I could muddle through and then maybe I could let Candace watch TV while I fell asleep in the early evening.

After a few quiet minutes Joe came back out with a bottle and three small glasses. Tapatio, said the bottle. It was tequila. Joe poured the drinks, doled them out, then lifted his glass high. "Death or glory," he said, downing it in one jerk of his head.

"Death or glory," said Mercedes, and she tipped her glass back.

"Death is gory," I said, and gulped mine down. It was smooth fire in my gullet. Joe immediately began pouring more.

Just before the third shot, I heard what I knew right away to be Candace's voice, in the way all parents know in such moments. She was crying terribly, sobs followed by a shriek, and then she was saying, "Daddy! Daddy!"

My heart left my chest. My face must have been something to see, because Mercedes didn't have to ask. She said, "Oh, Russ, go, go go."

I tore across the lawn, dodging the cactus, in through the front door, then right around the bend to Candace's room. I threw on the light and saw she was sitting cross-legged on the floor, her face red, eyes wet. She was breathing hard. "Daddy, Daddy, Daddy," she said, then huffed and huffed and sobbed on my shoulder as I picked her up.

"I know," I said, "I know. You're okay. I'm here. You're okay."

I walked over to the switch and put the light back out and lay her down, then climbed into bed with her. She curled into me. After a time, her choppy breathing smoothed out, her sobbing slowed.

I felt awful that she'd found herself alone. I was angry with myself for that. Alone or cold: those are the two states that I can't stand to think of her suffering. It kicks me in the stomach to think of it. I did not promise her it wouldn't happen again, because it's important to be realistic about such things. But I promised myself I'd try harder.

I lay listening to her breathe, and to the traffic, and the dogs. She slept, finally, without me ever knowing what it was that set her off. I drifted off, too.

In the morning, I woke in a panic and had to call in to say I'd be late.

"It's my daughter," I said.

Candace had always been a good sleeper, quick to go off and hard to wake, but that seemed to be gone. The next night, she again awoke frantic, and would fight sleep in the evenings that followed with a screaming desperation which frightened and frustrated me.

It wasn't until one evening, many weeks later, that she finally fell quietly asleep: in the back seat, as we went to pick a few things up at the store.

So began a period when, every night after dinner, I'd take her for a drive. We'd eat and I'd wash up, then maybe read a book with her or watch something, and then I'd put her in her PJs and we'd get into the car and go. She would start pointing out things she saw, or asking me questions about the things we passed, then she'd grow quiet, and soon, usually by the time we hit the limits of Yuma, she'd drift off.

It felt fragile to me, her sleep, so I'd drive around awhile longer. A lot of nights I'd head for a turnoff I'd found up in the hills, east of the city. Just a little spot where you can duck off the highway, a gravel patch that peeks from between some hills, back toward the city. I'd pull off and park there, and I'd listen to the radio softly.

I still believe in radio, in the waves that float through our lives, available for capture. A way to communicate, a way to pass information, a way to feel a part of human enterprise. Words and music. Everywhere I go I am aware that I am passing through radio signals, and that they are passing through me. I'm happy they're there, and that they're free.

What I found, sitting up there and scanning the dial, were signals rising up from Mexico. I do not speak Spanish, nor understand it, but I found these stations mesmerizing and, in a way, comforting. A world right there, next to me, that I did not know but which beat on anyway. It was the narcocorrido songs that caught my attention most: earnest, dramatic songs about the drug wars. Folk heroes. They seemed cut out of time, or as if I'd found myself in some pocket of the past. Parked up there, with a partial view of Yuma's twinkling lights, and the soft night air, Candace would sleep in her car seat, and I would sit and listen to that music, trying to imagine an outlaw's life.

A month passed, six weeks. I was beginning to despair a bit where Shona was concerned, thinking I'd misread her desire to be with me, but then she told me one night that she'd decided to come see us. It both surprised and pleased me.

"You mean that?" I said.

"Are you happy?" she asked.

"Jesus, Shon, I'm. Yes. When?"

"Second week of March," she said.

It wasn't so far off. Just a few weeks. I wanted to tidy up my life ahead of her arrival, so I cleaned the house top to bottom. I hung photos on the walls. I bought new cutlery. Got a haircut. Took Candace to a little salon and got her all cleaned up. I went to a mall and bought two new shirts for me and some new clothes for Candace. I put wine in the fridge, clean linen on the beds, and flowers in a pickle jar on the kitchen table.

Her trip took her through Los Angeles, with a connection to Yuma in a tiny prop plane that skimmed over the mountains. Candace and I waited in the small airport late that afternoon, me nervously watching every face coming through the gate. When I saw Shona, and she saw me, her eyes lit up and a small smile crept across her face—a smile like relief and mischief rolled together. We walked toward one another quickly. She looked good. Weary but healthy. I put my arms around her and my face over her shoulder and into her abundant hair. Her voice in my ear, saying to me, "I told you. I told you I'd come."

"Yes, you did." I pressed against her and I felt her back's long curve, felt her breathing.

Candace squealed a bit, standing at our feet. She tugged on Shona's jeans.

"She's been looking forward to this," I said. "She's made you gifts." They were scraps of paper she'd cut out into shapes like hearts and glued together, with crayon scrawls on them. They were welcome hearts, Candace said, and she carried them in a little Hello Kitty satchel she wore everywhere.

"I'll give them to you in the car," Candace said.

"Sounds good," Shona said, and knelt down for a hug. When she stood up again she looked right at me and she seemed almost giddy. "Yuma!"

"Yuma," I said. "Welcome. We're glad you're here."

"Well," she said, "show me Yuma."

I drove slowly down 32nd, past the airbase. It appeared busy. Silver contrails sutured the sky. The sand all around was a deep golden amber. The desert stretched out and disappeared, and the hills shimmered like blue smoke. I thought Yuma was showing its best aspect to Shona, and I hoped it was making an impression on her. In the passenger seat she smiled through her green-framed sunglasses.

That night I did not drive Candace around, but simply put her down to bed, and she chatted with her unicorns and bears for a long while. From her bedroom, Candace's voice was lazy and soft. I imagined sleep as a swimming pool, and my baby girl crouched on the edge, her toes curled over the lip, reluctant to slip in. Finally, finally, she was quiet. I hoped that meant she was over her sleeping troubles—that perhaps she'd been missing Shona, too, and insomnia was her way of expressing it.

Shona and I stood in the kitchen, slouched against the counters, talking in low tones. I kept moving in close, hooking a finger into the belt loops of her jeans. I did not wish to let her go. When we were sure Candace was asleep, we devoured one another, then fell into a deep, dumb sleep.

In the middle of the night, my lover woke and went to the kitchen. I heard the fridge door open. I got up, too, pulled on my jeans, and followed her. She was standing in front of the sink, drinking a bottle of beer.

"What's up?" I said.

"I was thirsty," she said, tilting the bottle and giving an impish little shrug. "Couldn't sleep."

"Maybe the time change," I said.

She had on blue underwear and my plaid shirt, open, her navel winking out at me. Her hair was a riot. She held the bottle out to me. "Sip?"

"I'll take my own," I said, opening the fridge and grabbing one.

She turned and looked at her dim reflection in the window over the sink. Outside, lights winked, windows glowed, lives were lived. A dog barking somewhere, and the persistent buzz of traffic on the Interstate. I placed my beer on the counter, moved in behind Shona, and wrapped one arm around her shoulders and the other around her waist. I looked at our reflection. She smiled.

"Look at that," I said. "We fit."

"We fit," she said, and leaned her head back. I squeezed a little tighter and she pushed back into me. Her warmth and her smell nearly knocked me down. My shirt hung down below her hips but I held her bare stomach. It was hot to the touch. I was so happy in that moment. I have trouble capturing it. I wanted to make everything last forever.

I thought to myself, here is the woman—what took you so long to find her? Here is the one who will give you a home, the one who will save you from drift, from aimlessness. Here is the woman who will know you and see your value, who will show it to you. Here she is, Russ, and you'd best not fuck this up.

"Come back to bed," I said.

"Will it be worth my while?" she asked.

"I believe it will," I said. And I believe it was.

In the morning, she was in a light mood. She sat at the kitchen table looking at her phone.

"Know what they call people from here?" she asked.

"No, what?"

"Yumans. Isn't that hilarious?"

"I hadn't heard that. We're surrounded by Yumans."

"They're everywhere!" she said, and then laughed. I laughed, too.

Candace, who was eating Cheerios, looked up and said, "Who is everywhere?" and seemed annoyed when we kept laughing.

We drove out into the desert that afternoon, just to have a look, then had dinner at a Mexican place downtown. I put Candace to bed and we watched a movie, but didn't make it to the end. Shona fell asleep on my shoulder and we had a quiet night, but made love in the morning and showered together before my little girl woke up. It was beginning to feel as though Shona had come to stay, but I was careful not to bring it up—I didn't want to hear otherwise.

Once the week began and I was back to work, Shona took it on herself to get to know Yuma a bit. I was hopeful that her aim was to become familiar with the place where she'd be living. She'd get up with me and drive me to the site—still out east of town—and then take my car for the day. She found a yoga studio called the Sea of Tranquility. She bought herself boots and jeans and cowboy shirts at a Western-wear shop. She went for a hike in the hills. She and Candace would come out at the end of the day to pick me up, then we'd go home and cook dinner together. Candace loved all this, the feeling of family, I guess you'd say, and just how much more lively the house was with Shona in it.

Toward the end of the week, with Shona's return to Ottawa the elephant in the room, my baby girl asked, out of the blue, "Sho-sho, do you live with us now?"

"Not yet," Shona said, her eyes on me. "I need to talk to your dad about that."

"Okay," I said, "let's talk about it."

"Okay," she said, "let's." She wore a funny grin that seemed to express excitement over the idea, while also gently mocking my serious tone. A dimple grew in her left cheek.

"We'd love you to. I think you know that," I said. "I know there are questions to answer, things to work out. But it's been so good having you here. I'd like this to go on."

"Me too, Russ," she said. "I think this is what I want."

I became all tensed up—my eyes, my throat, my chest. I was happy she'd said that, happy she'd been feeling about the week the same way I had. "Okay," I said, "okay. Where do we start?"

She stood and held her arms out. I stood and moved into her and we hugged.

"I guess we just. Just start," she said.

And that's what we did. She extended her stay into April, and we went on living that life. She started to have some say in small things, like the colour of the placemats I bought, and the decision to put Candace in swimming lessons down at the Y. It seemed like she was taking her first, early steps into what would become our home.

What she hadn't told me was that she'd been having trouble sleeping since she arrived. Spent the nights lying awake next to me and trying not to toss too much. Perhaps it was the decision to stay: trying to make it, and then, having made it, experiencing some doubts. I missed it all, was oblivious. I assumed her lack of rest was due to the early mornings, getting me to the job site so she could have the car. Shona's more of a night person than a morning one. But I should have known it meant something when the skin beneath her eyes darkened. I think I chose not to.

She flew back to Ottawa, *to settle things* was how she put it, and figured she'd be gone a month before joining us in a more permanent way. We drove her to the airport in the early morning of a Saturday, stood by the fence, and waved as her little plane lifted away.

We spoke each night after she left, but not until Candace and I had done our driving routine, which was once again proving necessary. I'd sit in the driver's seat, listening to the narcocorridos as winged things clicked against the windshield, until my girl's breathing slowed. When we got back to the house, I'd tuck her into bed and then dial Shona's phone. Sometimes we'd talk an hour, and sometimes we'd chat five minutes, but hearing her—telling her I missed her, hearing her tell me the same—I'd feel good about what lay ahead for us.

By the time Shona returned, in May, it was beginning to get well and truly hot. She shipped me a couple of boxes of her things, then arrived with two overloaded suitcases. She'd stored everything else in her sister's basement in Ottawa.

"It was kind of great to pare down," she told me. "Who needs all that stuff?"

We had a little party—for its own sake, I suppose, but also to celebrate Shona's decision to stay. Joe and Mercedes came. They were something like friends to me now, and I wanted to share my happiness with them. Their little ones played with Candace in my tiny yard while the four of us sat laughing and drinking in lawn chairs. The sky went dusky and I plugged in a string of lights I'd hung along the fence. "Fancy!" said Shona.

I cooked chicken and corn on a little hibachi atop the picnic table, and we ate on paper plates. Shona had bought a tray of cupcakes at the Walmart. The kids raced around, kicked a ball, walked dolls through the dry grass and sand. Then it got late, and though I was wobbly, I felt the tug of responsibility to get Candace to bed.

Shona knew, she could see it in the way I was watching my daughter through the little kitchen window as I put the paper plates in the trash and scrubbed the things I'd used to cook the chicken. She read me so well. "Can I get Candace ready for bed?" she asked. "I'd like to do that."

"She'd love that."

"Will she make a fuss over Sonny and Annie still being up?" I'd already explained to her about the approach Joe and Mercedes took to bedtime for their kids.

"I think having you get her ready will offset that," I said.

Shona kissed me quickly on the mouth and gave me a look with her hazel eyes that seemed to hold a promise in it. She then called Candace in, had her say goodnight to her friends, and took her by the hand and led her into the bathroom. As they walked by me, my daughter gave me a conspiratorial look. It was a look that said, *Look how I have captured her for you.* She loved Shona. I could see that. And what wasn't to love?

They were talking. I could not hear what they were saying, but there was laughing, and some serious conversation, too. After they moved into my little girl's bedroom and a nightshirt was slipped over Candace's head, Shona began to read to her. I could hear the easy, measured tones of a storybook in her voice.

"Sho-sho read the paper-princess story," Candace said, when I went in to kiss her goodnight.

"Did she like it? Did she do a good job?"

"Yes," they both said.

The room was warm. It was full of them. The light came from a lamp with a pink shade, made everything feel close and safe. We all smiled. Things felt so good, like they lined up the way I had hoped they would. It seemed Candace felt safe, felt she was home—and because she felt it, I felt it, too. Something was taking root in the desert, the accidental charge of life suddenly visiting us. I meant to capture it, to harness and hold it.

Shona sat on the side of the bed. I stood over her, smelled the fruity heat of her head. I couldn't see her face but I could still feel the smile there. Candace's eyes were so narrow they were almost shut, and her breathing was slow.

"How do you like having Shona tuck you in?" I asked.

"Can she do it tomorrow?"

"I guess I have my answer," I said, and we laughed.

We kissed Candace goodnight and switched out her light. She was asleep before we closed her door, I think. Then we rejoined our friends in the yard. Sonny had fallen asleep in Mercedes's lap. Annabel sat cross-legged at Joe's feet, telling him a story about a queen who lived up among the stars, which were beginning to make themselves visible over our heads. The light turned a deep blue and soon Annabel was asleep, too. We adults got high and laughed quietly. Tears came to my eyes as I inventoried my luck.

We're always making decisions, and then following through on them, without ever truly believing in their wisdom or suitability. It might be that's where Shona found herself: she was content, primarily, just to have a path to follow for a time. I don't quite know. She's never said so to me. She seemed happy enough. But maybe that's what I wanted to see. Piecing together things now, I am able to imagine that she couldn't quell some yearning, or doubt, or small, nagging objections. There was something she missed—something that wasn't in Yuma.

Meanwhile, I had got it in my head that we were on the edge of a new period of our lives, one that felt to me open, bright, and thrilling. Those were days of gorgeous desert sunrises, the new light over the east throwing its spectacular neon arms through the window, the smell of coffee, the sound of the dogs as they were roused. Shona had lucked into work leading classes at the Sea of Tranquility. It was just three of them a week, but she also got on the odd shift waiting tables at the Red Lobster. It had been so long since I'd even thought about the radio job that I began to see myself only as a labourer on road crews. It no longer felt like a temporary thing, and that was all right. I had Candace, I had Shona, and our little house, and friends to share a drink and a smoke.

Happiness was a recognizable thing. I looked at Shona as a source of it—or rather, I looked at the life we had, and would have, as a thing that might invite happiness in a more reliable way. And there was Candace, whose thoughts and actions fascinated and excited me even as they nudged me toward a sadness at the thought that she'd one day up and leave, to start her own life without me.

On all counts, I continued to view happiness as a thing that blesses us intermittently—a periodic dusting of gold down over our lives—and not as a thing to which we are entitled at all hours, every day. I did not believe it possible to banish sadness completely from one's life, nor did I think it desirable to do so. Sadness, I thought, was a reasonable and healthy response to a frequently sad world. I still think that.

Shona saw things a bit differently, I can tell you now. She once told me that anything that doesn't make you happy can and should be jettisoned from your life; that she could be happy from the moment she woke up until she fell asleep again, and that her dreams should be pleasant, too. And every day that this wasn't the case frustrated and upset her, made her look for things to change, in order to bring about a perfect state.

It was for this reason, I think, that her sadness came dressed like anger. Whereas mine, when it came, was more of a sloped-shouldered resignation. I could not tell you, given our approaches, which of us was better prepared for all of life's tiny assaults.

One Saturday, we found ourselves in the car before dawn. Candace was wrapped in a blanket and strapped into her seat in the back. Shona, in denim and fleece, dozed in the passenger seat, her head resting on the window, padded only by a balled-up nylon jacket.

We were following Mercedes and Joe and their kids out to the Imperial Sand Dunes. Joe said there was nothing like them. After an hour's drive, he said, we could walk on the surface of the moon.

The plan was to time a hike so that we could have a picnic breakfast and watch the sun come up over the dunes, then be back in our cars and headed home before the day's heat really hit. We crossed over into California on Interstate 8, then followed Mercedes and Joe's aging Chevy Tahoe north. Outside the car there was nothing. The world was confined to my high beams: a small, concentrated spray of light on the straight road, barren space just to either side. There were no businesses, no houses. It was blacktop and empty sand and nothing more.

We came to another highway and followed it west. Before long I could see the Tahoe's lights flashing staccato as Joe tapped the brakes. He pulled off the highway, onto the flat, sandy shoulder, and into a space marked by nothing but the tracks of vehicles that had been there before. He shut off his engine. There was nothing else around. No cars, no buildings, no people.

The dunes ran in a sandy gash from the northwest to the southeast, from the Salton Sea to Mexico, a shifting ocean of sand, hillocks, and swales remade daily by the wind. At the southern end they were cut by Interstate 8 and cross-hatched by a stretch of border fence. There, white SUVs patrolled and recreational off-roaders blazed. The area from where we had come, toward the northern end, off 78, was closed to off-road traffic. It was, as Joe promised, an alluringly desolate and lunar place.

We were nearing the lip of day when we stopped. The light was just beginning to seep above the horizon, back over the way we'd come. Shona woke when I stopped the car. I opened the back door and spoke gently to Candace, to wake her.

Mercedes was putting on a backpack while Joe let Annabel and Sonny out of their seats. Their faces were sleepy. Sonny held a little plush cat by the paw, dangling it. "We'd better leave Kit-Kit here," Joe said to him, "so we don't lose him."

"He can protect the truck," Sonny said in his small, eager voice.

"That's right."

The air was dry and cool. Only a small breeze swept us, but you could hear it clearly, raking over the sand.

Joe approached, a sort of backpack-cooler over his shoulders. "How was the drive?" he asked me. "Did Candace sleep?"

"They both did," I said, and Shona laughed. "It was great."

"There's kind of a trail from here," Joe said. "If we follow that for twenty minutes we should find a nice spot to stop and eat." Then he turned to his kids. "Everybody hungry?"

They nodded slowly. Annabel shyly slipped behind Mercedes's legs.

The trail, such as it was, was a narrow, dusty line somewhat beaten by shoe prints. We walked single file. Mercedes took the lead, then Joe. The three children followed, intermingling in a way that made me happy to see. Then Shona and me.

Five minutes in and our shoes were filled with sand. It was remarkable, the way our feet would sink in only so far, then find something like firm ground. It was like walking on an enormous beach, I suppose, above the waterline, except there was no water. I could feel the effort in the muscles of my calves and hips. I walked with my head down.

We paused and I had a chance to look up, back to the east. The faint pre-dawn light was leaking over the waves and dips of sand. There were no artificial lights, no signs of life, no vegetation save the odd lonely bush.

"Just ahead," Mercedes said. "There's a kind of a slope over that way. We can put a blanket down and eat."

The spot she indicated was inclined toward the east, forming a natural theatre from which we might watch the day begin. The sand was cool and chalky. Mercedes pulled a rolled-up blanket from her pack and laid it out, and Joe slipped his pack off and unzipped it. The kids sat on their knees as he handed them juice boxes.

We whispered when we spoke. I'm not sure why, except to say that it felt as though some degree of reverence was appropriate. When someone's voice rose, usually one of the kids', the sand had a way of swallowing the sound. *Like snow does*, I thought.

Mercedes then handed out egg sandwiches and fried potato patties while Joe distributed the contents of a coffee Thermos. The sky lightened perceptibly as we sat and ate.

"You have to admire that landscape," Joe said, indicating it with his plastic cup of coffee.

"It's such a strange and beautiful place, isn't it?" said Shona.

The kids were standing, twirling on their feet in the sand, corkscrewing themselves downward, filling their shoes.

"There's more coffee if you want it," Mercedes said.

It was a nice moment, sitting there anticipating the sun. Every once in a while the wind gave the smallest gust and kicked grains of sand against our cheeks. The smell was something I have trouble describing, something between charcoal and warm pavement. A grand moment was coming and we didn't want to miss it. But neither was there any particular hurry. We were at rest, among easy company. The only sounds were of a bit of wind, our sparse chatter, the voices of our children.

An orange wedge suddenly appeared above a tall ridge of dunes.

Joe stood. "Welcome to Saturday," he said.

Molten smudges of light began pouring over the horizon and running toward us, and the wedge quickly became a ball. It was an incredible sight. It looked like the beginning of the world. Or the end of it, I suppose.

I swallowed my coffee and stood next to Joe, one hand on my hip. Shona stood, too, and put her arms around my waist. "God," she said. "I'm no morning person, but Jesus."

"How do you feel now about being woken up so early?" I asked.

"Oh, yeah," she said, "totally worth it."

The sun lit us up as it sprung up over the sand. I could feel the air getting warmer immediately. Everything was on fire. A cauldron from the earth's heart had been tipped and its contents were flowing toward us. We were of the morning. And then we were in it. The day breaking over the world was enormous.

"Candace," I said, "are you watching? Do you see the sun coming up?"

I wanted to share it with her, hoped maybe to create some memory: that time we watched the sun come up over the Imperial Sand Dunes.

She did not answer me.

"Candace?"

Nothing. I don't know if it requires having a child of your own to imagine my terror. I suspect it does. Think of it: your child there, and then gone.

"Candace," I said again, trying to moderate the panic I knew had crept into my voice. I turned fully around and saw only Annabel and Sonny. "Where is Candace?" I said, not at all calmly, though I knew I ought not alarm them.

Shona's antennae picked up all this, and she said, "Oh Jesus. Candace! Candace!"

"She can't have gone anywhere," said Joe. "There's nowhere to go around here. Look. There's nowhere."

He was right, but there was also no Candace. We fanned out and began turning in circles, all of us except the other children, who stood with their hands to their mouths and their shoulders balled up, afraid.

I looked at Annabel and Sonny. "Did you see her?" I asked.

They shook her tiny heads no, their eyes growing wider with fear.

"Candace, baby, where have you gone to?" said Mercedes.

I could not imagine where she could be. There were no trees, no rocks—nothing, as Joe had said, to hide behind. Had the sand swallowed her up? Had something silently carried her off? I felt my body go cold, my limbs and digits taking on a numb rigidity at precisely the moment I needed them to be most agile.

"Candace!" I shouted. "Candace!"

I broke into a run, away from the blanket, away from the rising sun, which I could feel on my back and shoulders. It was the only direction to go, since I had not seen her in front of us, and the trail was clear in both directions. I ran west into the nothingness, my knees high, the sand pulling me downward. Shona ran behind me, calling to Candace, calling to me.

I stopped running a moment, just to breathe, and had an instant of strange clarity. I could see beyond my own life, to a time when we no longer existed, a time when all we were and all we'd had was lost, when all that was left was the air and light encircling us. I don't know what brought it on, except that strange landscape, and the thought of my daughter being gone.

I snapped back to the immediate world when Shona called my name again. I turned and saw she'd fallen and was reaching down to her right ankle. She had misstepped, found something beneath the surface of the sand, and turned her ankle over.

"Shon," I said.

She sat kind of crumpled in the dust, lit from behind, her head haloed by the sun. She was taking these sorts of hiccupy breaths and her hair was strung across her face.

"Baby," I said, "I can't help you right now. Stay put there. You're fine." And she looked at me quizzically, her cheeks reddened with pain, and likely her vision gone a bit soft. "I have to find her," I said.

And I did not help Shona to her feet.

The moment didn't need to be a significant one. I see that now. I might even have seen it then. But I chose to make it significant. Willed it to be so. Made of it an opportunity to plainly display the order of things, the hierarchy I planned to defend and reinforce in my life.

Shona, I'd said with my eyes and with my actions, *you are wonderful, but you will never be anything close in importance as my little girl. And if that isn't acceptable to you, you can rest there in the dust eternally, for all I care.*

And in the hurt way in which she looked at me before I turned my shoulders away from her, I saw that Shona understood all of this, as clearly as if I'd spoken it.

I continued on toward my own long shadow, calling my daughter's name. Wandered for many more minutes. I turned back, only once, to see that Shona had gotten to her feet, unsteadily.

I kept walking toward the west until I came to a small ridge. There was a dark space beyond it, a cool depression that I hadn't seen until I was right atop it. It was perhaps twenty feet across, and nearly as deep. Just a little hole in the dunes, caused by who knows what.

And down there, in the bowl of sand, sat Candace. She lay curled in the bottom of it, untouched by the sun.

"Candace, baby!" I shouted.

"Hi, Daddy."

I heard the voices of the others calling my name now.

"Here," I called. "She's here!"

I slid on my heels and my palms down the side of the bowl and then crawled over to her. I grabbed her and pulled her into my chest.

"Candace, baby, are you okay? What are you doing? We've been calling you."

"I didn't hear you."

"My God, I thought you were lost."

"I was just here," she said.

The others appeared at the rim, looking down at us.

"She's all right?" Joe asked.

"She's okay," I said.

Mercedes said, "Oh, thank God."

"Look, Dad," Candace said, indicating the walls around us, "it's like a fort." She was not in the least bit distressed.

"You scared the wits out of me, baby. Don't you wander off like that."

"I wanted to see how far the sun got," she said.

"Come on out," I said.

With some effort, and some help, we climbed out of that depression and back up to where the sun was.

Shona was hobbled. She held her right heel off the ground and was putting her weight on her left.

"Sorry, Shon," I said, nodding at it. I was apologizing, at least partially, for something other than her physical injury. We both felt that.

"I understand," she said. "I'll be okay."

Because what else was there to say?

She put her arm over my shoulder and I helped her walk slowly back toward the blanket. There, I helped Joe and Mercedes gather the breakfast things, and then we went back up the trail to the cars.

We were different people, suddenly. The children, even Candace, carried on as though nothing had happened. But Mercedes, I could see, was a bit shaken by what had occurred. She watched her two with an extra bit of alertness.

As we walked, Joe said to me, "Bit of a scare, huh, Russ? You okay?"

"Sure," I said. "All's well."

Shona grunted a bit as she put weight on her foot.

We drove back east. The rim of the world was aflame. The road was on fire. The hood was on fire. I squinted and pulled down the sunshade, before finally putting my faith in geometry—in the road's straightness across the earth's gently curved face.

Candace peppered us with questions such as "Where are the animals?" and "What's under the sand?" I tried my best to address them with short answers, in order to preserve the overriding silence, which I felt was the only thing keeping Shona from beginning an uncomfortable conversation.

Shona rode with her right foot up on the dash, looking out the window at the brightening world.

When Candace's questions tapered off and then stopped altogether, I felt a tightness, a hesitation. Quietly panicking, I sped up and passed Mercedes and Joe. It was an act of aggression and desperation, and I was sorry for it even as I executed it. It was as if I were attempting to speed away from what had happened, as though if enough distance was traversed in a short enough period of time I could reverse the events of the morning thus far.

I turned on the radio and found a classic rock station from California, its signal cascading over the dunes and the tarmac and into the rising sun. On came the opening salvo of "Seven Wonders" by Fleetwood Mac. It came over me like unearned relief. I turned it up, way up. We looked out our respective windows—Candace, Shona, and me— and were overwhelmed by the song's shimmering cocaine opulence, its incandescent beauty. *A certain time, a certain place*, cooed Stevie Nicks. I have trouble conveying just how at odds the song was with the mood within the car, but I relied on it to buy me a few more minutes of non-conversation.

When it was over, a commercial began and Shona reached for the knob. She turned the sound down and said to me, "I didn't know you liked Fleetwood Mac."

"I believe that everybody, somewhere within themselves, loves Fleetwood Mac," I said.

I wondered then what made me the person I was. I felt unhooked from almost everything I had ever known.

Once home, Shona took some painkillers and sat on the couch with a bag of frozen peas on her ankle, sipping tea and checking her phone.

"Anything I can get you?" I asked her.

"I'm fine, Russ," she said. There was a flatness to her that I couldn't miss.

She had an evening shift at the Red Lobster, which I welcomed. I thought it would give us a bit of time to pull back from a precipice. I helped her wrap the ankle up tight so she could walk on it. She popped a couple of Advils and pulled her stockings over the bandage.

"You sure you'll be okay?" I asked her.

"Sure. Just have a bottle of wine waiting for when I'm done," she said.

"You bet I will," I said.

It was nearly midnight when she got back. I'd had a quiet afternoon and evening with Candace. We'd had hot dogs for dinner, and when I put her to bed, she went down quickly. Then I turned on the TV, flicked around, grew bored, and switched it off. I opened some wine, lay in the dark with the bedroom window open, and finished the bottle, just thinking, just talking to myself. I dozed off, woke, dozed some more.

Shona stood in the bedroom doorway. "Russ?" she said.

I started awake but tried to pretend I hadn't been asleep. "Just lying here, baby," I said. "How'd it go? How's the ankle?"

"I got through it," she said. "I'm gonna hop in the shower now."

I lay a little longer in the dark, listening to the running water and the usual outside hum of traffic and dogs, then walked to the kitchen and took a wineglass off the shelf for Shona. I opened another three-dollar bottle of California red, filled her glass to the brim, sipped a bit off, and carried it to the bathroom. I knocked gently, too gently for Shona to hear it in the shower, and pushed the door open.

"Hey there," I said, so that I wouldn't startle her.

"Hey, hey," she said.

I pushed the shower curtain aside and poked my head in. She was slick and red, the water running in a hundred different streams all down her body. I looked down at her ankle, which was red and puffy and would turn purple and black the next day. Then I looked back at her face. She frowned theatrically. I handed her the wine.

"Thank you," she said, and took a big gulp, then handed it back to me. "Just gotta wash my hair."

I put the glass on the counter and walked out, back to the bedroom.

She came out many minutes later, wrapped in a towel. "I just had one of those moments, you know," she said. "When you kind of don't know how you got here?"

I was lying on the bed in the dark again. "Got here?"

She switched on the little bedside lamp. "Like, Yuma. What am I doing here?" And she laughed, to show me she wasn't sad or angry.

"You're with me."

"Right. I know. Life's funny."

"That hurts a bit," I said.

"You're just not the kind of man I ever pictured myself with."

"I'm not supposed to find that hurtful?"

"It just is. It's a thing that is. You don't have to think of it as hurtful, unless you want to. And you seem to want to."

I poured myself more wine. She did the same, after downing the rest of her glass. I was beginning to recognize the parameters of the conversation, its scale, its shape. It wasn't just about her ankle. Or about Yuma.

She sat on the bed, cross-legged, and ran a towel over her hair. She smelled like a tropical greenhouse.

"Maybe I just see us differently than you do," I said.

"I think that's obvious, baby. We don't see the world just the same way. You're stern so much of the time, like you don't trust happiness."

"The truth is I'm not even sure I know what it is," I said.

"It means feeling good, you sweet fool."

"Things that don't feel good can also be good for you. That's something I believe. Responsibilities."

"But too many of those things?"

"How do you know how many is too many? How do you know when something isn't going to be good for you, which things to keep working for?"

Those were real questions I asked myself from time to time.

"It's okay to try things out, Russ. To see where they go. It's okay to be unsure, then try anyway, then decide it isn't the thing you need. Why wouldn't we do the things that make us happiest?"

I realized then that she'd been seeing my willingness to pull up stakes—Ottawa, Watertown, Yuma—as an indication that I approached life as she did. She thought that I had been exchanging one life for another, in order to be happy.

But the truth was I wanted constancy. To always to have my people in my life. Candace. Shona. In changing my surroundings, I was only trying to find the right venue for us to begin our efforts in earnest. I wanted to find the one permanent place.

I sighed and shifted, tilted my head back, squeezed my eyes shut a moment.

"I'm close to drunk," I said. "Join me?"

"I'm getting there," she said, taking another gulp.

I was glad to hear it, though the wine wasn't delivering me the sense of ease I'd hoped it would. I was on edge, and I knew she sensed that. I hoped more wine would loosen us up.

Everything changes. I forget that from time to time. I had certainly forgotten it with respect to Shona. I'd let myself believe we'd arrived at a lovely, endless plateau. I was lulled into believing we'd left change behind us.

She was looking at the bottom of her glass. "Russ," she said. "What a day."

"Truth. Can we forget it?"

"No. But we can maybe improve the ending a bit."

"What do you want, Shona?" I sat up and put my face close to hers. "Tell me what you want, baby."

She drained her glass, then looked at me and smiled. "I want you to fuck me like I deserve it," she said.

"You do."

"Then fuck me like you deserve it."

She shed her towel and moved on top of me.

We were not young, but we were not dead. Our skin still invited touch. She was furious. I was on fire.

It reminded me of the first time we were together, when our recklessness imperfectly reflected our bodies' desperation, expressed our lurking suspicions that we'd already become old before we'd even had a chance to feel young, that we'd already known our allotments of tenderness, of sweetness, of moist, red lust. It was obvious to me then, that first time, that she saw me as I saw myself in infrequent, optimistic, usually drunken moments. I'd found my best reflection, and she was beautiful. I never wanted it to end.

This time, the desperation had a different quality. For me, it was one of trying to claw something back. For her, it was one of finality, of fighting for breath, of emerging, of finding a way out from beneath a weight. We bit and pulled and struggled. I didn't know if it was to be our last time—not with certainty, though the fear was there. I was always concerned that she'd wise up and move past me, but now it was more immediate, sadder and angrier and more frantic. I was fighting for her.

As it happened, it wasn't our last time. We entwined like that almost nightly for two weeks. When we weren't in bed, we got along amiably, though I became aware that we spoke in different terms, avoiding all talk of the future, using words to place a small buffer between our lives. The basic truth of us had been altered, and I knew that Shona, in her heart, was bound for elsewhere.

The days grew hotter and the nights more still, and the stars seemed to burn more intensely. The mounting heat and the breathless evenings rubbed up against the new, strange distance that had crept between us to create something spiky, something that threatened to combust. It was, for those weeks, our bodies which burned. There was a permanent sheen on my brow, and the dry air made her hair feel brittle. But that did not prevent me from wanting to sink my hands deep into it, my face, my nose.

Our daytime selves, though, were going to have to be reckoned with sooner or later. We both knew it. The wide-awake versions of us, with so many practical concerns in mind and so many sober hours to contend with, would be the ones making the decisions. And Shona's daytime self seemed, to me, completely resigned to the end of whatever it was we had.

There was no descent into acrimony—a small thing of which I am nonetheless proud. I have never sought to turn love to hate with anyone I've ever known, including Candace's mother. I just never saw that as desirable. I understand, of course, that people don't just look at the one they love and say, *One day I'll hate her*. Love runs its course, and then they find something much different residing in their heart.

My heart remained steady, and I think Shona's did, too; at least, I believe it did not do a complete reversal. She still felt tenderness toward me, still had access to that place in her heart she'd once put me. But now she knew what she was up against. She would never be the only girl in my heart, would never represent my sole concern. Most of us would like to think of ourselves as someone's sole concern, I think that's normal. And I expect it scared her, showed her all at once just how vulnerable she was. Her reaction was to pull back, to protect herself.

None of this was said aloud. There was no explicit conversation about us drifting apart. She did not tell me, *Russ, I'm having doubts.* Instead, it was in the set of her shoulders, in the avoided instances of contact. There were no more hands on my back as I stood in the kitchen, no pecks on the cheek. I noticed such things because they had once been so abundant.

What I should have done was pushed. I see that now. I don't know if it would have swayed her, but at least I'd have tried.

The end came on a Monday evening. We'd put Candace to bed and were sitting on chairs in the kitchen, talking about what we'd have for dinner the rest of the week. It was such a regular conversation. Just a man and a woman discussing groceries. Then there was a lull.

"Russ, I don't think I can keep doing this."

"Doing what?"

She put her elbows on the table and put her head in her hands. "I'm sorry. I wanted us to work. But if I'm being honest, it's not. It's just not working for me. And I don't believe it will."

"So. You're, uh. You're going? You're going to leave?"

"It can't seem sudden to you, babe," she said, lifting her eyes to me. "It hasn't felt right, has it?"

"I figured growing pains."

"Baby."

"I had dreams of marrying you."

"You're going to be okay. Do you hear me? I promise you're going to be okay. You'll always have her."

I cried then. Shona took me to bed and we lay there and held one another, which was strange and comforting and painful at once.

In the morning, she simply left. She kissed Candace on the forehead and me on the mouth, touched my face, and was gone in the taxi before I could even get my bearings. She flew out of Yuma, and I doubt she will ever return there. From what I understand, she stayed in Ottawa for a time before heading to Toronto, where she waits tables when she isn't teaching yoga. I do not know if she is attached. I do not believe she has any children.

Why do we have so much trouble knowing what we want? Or keeping it once we do know?

I had once believed—sincerely and fervently—that I wanted Yuma as a home, but it began looking quite different to me in the wake of Shona's departure. A place still on the edge, yes, but maybe too much so. Too barren, too open, too spare. It was a desert town full of itinerants and dogs. It was a place to be, but not a place to stay. It just wasn't a home of any kind, not for me; and though I was glad Candace could say, later in her life, *I lived in Arizona,* it wasn't the home I wanted for her either.

I did not sleep well after Shona flew away. Yuma had become a venue of loss for me, and I was done with it. I needed only to settle the question of where to be next. And because I could come up with no new answers, I fell back on an old one.

When Candace was a baby and her mother and I were still together, we lived in eastern Ontario, in rural idyll.

There was a station in Kemptville where I kept things running as best as possible with limited resources. We did farm reports and played Top 40 music, ran syndicated programming overnight from seven to five. My commute into town took me ten minutes, down a few gravel roads and a two-lane highway that snaked along next to the South Branch of the Rideau River. We had a staff of six. The office administrator also handled ad accounts. The custodian hosted the noon show.

I returned each evening to our two treed acres and the slumping ranch-style house thereupon, to my wife and our baby. On spring nights the peepers sent up a chorus from the fields and wetlands, and in the fall we'd wake at first light to the sound of the hunters' rifles. It was a small, not unenjoyable life.

But it hadn't been enough to hold off the things lurking in our margins. Our marriage exploded, and then my wife went away, and I found myself bringing up Candace by myself. It was a hard few years, I'll admit.

Yet despite all that, for me eastern Ontario retained an Edenic quality, as sheltered and quiet and desirable. There was an honesty about the place and the people there. A straightforwardness. I still had friends there, and contacts. I was still well thought of. People were eager to help me resettle, to beat life into some sort of shape that might aid me and nurture Candace. It felt for all the world that a second crack at a life there would be a good thing.

So Kemptville was where we began anew. In the back of my mind, of course, I knew that I was trying to resettle not only into an old place, but into the person I had once been, before Yuma, before Shona. Such is a faulty premise upon which to build a life, but I didn't see any other choice.

I was hired on at the Home Hardware, in the yard and working the contractors' counter. I also made some overtures to my old employers at the station. *If anything opens up*, they said, and I believe they were sincere.

For a few months, we rented a damp and sour townhouse on the edge of town. Then I put some money down on a bungalow in the country, at the edge of what had been a pine plantation. The house occupied a corner lot where two concessions met. Behind, to the east, lay empty fields gone to hay. Regularly spaced rows of mast-straight red pines ran to the south. In among them had grown thickets of cedar and some maple. It was August, sweet-smelling and hot, by the time we moved in. Candace was due to begin kindergarten in September. We had a month to make a home, just the two of us.

Next door, perhaps two hundred yards away, lay a brick house, similarly nestled among the shading trees. It was owned by the Meachams, Cal and Julie. Cal I'd known a bit, once upon a time. He drove a snowplow for the township. Julie taught at the high school. Their daughter was in her teens, and in the back of my mind I flagged her as a potential babysitter, if I ever again had a need for one.

Autumn dropped suddenly, in late September, the world going rust-coloured. Candace was in the middle of a growth spurt, stretching out her limbs, taking her from the round little girl I'd known into a whippet-lean kid, with just her apple-cheeked grin to remind me of the bundle she'd only recently been. I found her a snowsuit at the Salvation Army, hoped she wouldn't outgrow it in that first winter.

Yuma, though never all that far from my mind, was starting to feel like a distant memory. I wondered if I'd ever know anything like it again. I doubted it, if I was being honest with myself.

I thought, though, that Candace and I might have something good in Kemptville: fine lives which left us content, and not impacted by tragedy. Cal and Julie had us over from time to time for barbecues and, once winter settled in, to watch Saturday-evening hockey on their big screen, eating stews made of the game Cal had taken over the fall.

By the time the snow fell, we thought we had ourselves something like a home. But then Christmas passed, and January was hard. Mountains of snow, worse than I'd remembered, with a half-dozen snow days that shut down the school buses, sending me scrambling to make arrangements. The house was terribly drafty. In some rooms it felt as though someone had left a window open. I brought home parabolic space heaters from the hardware store, one for each room, two in the kitchen. Candace wore leggings beneath her pants, and heavy fleece pyjamas with socks. In the mornings, while I waited for the coffee maker, I stood blowing into my cupped hands and wiggling my toes in my wool socks.

One night in the middle of February, I woke around two with an acrid smell in my mouth and nose. I knew immediately what it was, and did not check to be sure. I went to Candace and I picked her up, along with the stuffed menagerie she was clutching in her arms. I gathered her to me and made my way to the front door, stuffed animals spilling to the floor as we went. I could see a glow coming from the back room, and heard a low roaring sound, and the sound and the light were creeping toward the kitchen with a dreadful sort of desire.

Candace woke in my arms and began sobbing, sensing my panic, the way children can. I grabbed our coats on our way out the door, wrapped her in hers, and put her in the car. I started the engine and turned the heat all the way up, for it was a bitterly cold night, and backed the car down the lane until it was out on the edge of the gravel road. There, I pulled my coat on and told Candace that everything was okay, everything would be fine, just please sit tight. Then I walked toward the house to see if anything could be done. But of course nothing could.

Flames had reached the roof. The living room windows were glowing orange, and something—perhaps paint cans in the garage—was popping like dried kernels. I ran through the trees and snow to the Meachams'. Their garage light, hooked up to a motion sensor, flared on, and Homer, their German shepherd, began to bark. I pounded on their front door, and when Julie Meacham answered in a robe, I said, "My house is on fire. Could you call it in?"

"Oh my God, of course," she said. "Candace?"

"With me. She's all right. We're all right."

Then I stood in the lane. Candace was behind me, in the idling car, probably needing me, needing to be reassured. But I kept on standing alone there, feeling as though I was losing my mind. It was hard to understand what was happening in front of me, even as I witnessed it. Our entire material life was now fuel. Books and clothes. Tools. Candace's toys. I wondered what, in this life, would prove durable.

The trucks came shortly, two of them, from Kemptville. "These goddamn prefabs are made of paper," I heard one of the firefighters say, and what I witnessed bore that out. Even as I stood in the lane, people in thick uniforms and gear racing about me, the house was completely consumed. The cedar hedge to the north of the little house caught, and it began to fizzle and pop, as did a maple in the yard whose branches hung over the roof, its limbs soon falling from it into the blaze. Embers drifted up toward the needles of the pines, and I thought it only a matter of moments before we had a forest fire on our hands.

But that never came about. After a time, I went to the car and got in the back seat with my baby. I held her and we cried together and I said, "The important thing is that you're not hurt. You're okay. We're okay." I could feel the heat on my face and her tears falling onto me.

The police put us in a motel on the other side of the highway. I lay with Candace, and she cried and asked me questions for which I had no answers. Eventually we got some sleep, though not much.

In the morning, I drove us out to the house to survey the damage. Along the way, the bare trees looked like cut crystal as the sun shone through the frost which had settled there in the night. The sky was high and bright, and the snow sparkled. Were it not for our circumstances, I'd have seen beauty in all of it.

There was still smoke rising from the ashes when I pulled into the long drive, tight against the row of cedars. Some of them had burned to their stumps. I sat there a moment, looking at the way the absence of the house changed the view of the property and the trees, the fields beyond. It was a pretty spot, I realized, one that had been profaned when the bungalow was dropped there. I tried to imagine what might rise next, if anything, and in that moment I knew I wouldn't have the strength to rebuild. I'd let the bank and the insurance company work out what to do with it.

Candace sat in the back seat, hugging her unicorn and her Hello Kitty. She did not ask to come out of the car. In fact, she appeared to shrink when I looked at her, as though worried I'd ask her to come out with me.

"I'll be just over there," I said, looking back at her over my shoulder. "Will you be okay here? For a minute?"

She nodded.

Leaving the car running with the heat turned all the way up, I stepped out and pulled on my gloves. It was an arctic morning, twenty below, and the air stung my nostrils, lashed my face. I walked over to the house, stepping over ruts and tire tracks, over the tree limbs that had fallen, bare and singed. The house was a blackened heap. There were patches, less burned, where I recognized features, and in the northeast corner a part of the roof was still held up by two partial walls, burned down to the studs but resilient. The smell of burned wood, plastic, chemically treated material, was overwhelming. I held my arm over my face.

The garage, which had been a shoddy addition to the original structure, was gone altogether. The siding on the garden shed, thirty feet away from the house, was melted and disfigured. Everywhere, the water from the firefighters' hoses had refrozen into smooth shapes, coating the ground, filigreeing the edges of scorched things.

There were objects I recognized peeking from the mess, but they were sullied, or halved, or made grotesque. I saw a coffee mug with a football helmet on it, fused to a blob of misshapen metal which used to be a Thermos. I saw bits of colour that appeared to have been toys. I saw furniture without upholstery. Cutlery, twisted and maimed.

The sheer, useless mass of it all overwhelmed me.

I kicked over a piece of blackened drywall, heavy and frozen, from what I believe was the wall separating the kitchen from the living room. There had been a bookshelf there, but I could see no trace of that. Under the Gyproc I discovered a banker's box that had sat on the lowest shelf. Half of the box was more or less gone, scorched and then dissolved by the hoses' water, but when I flipped the lid open, the contents were still recognizable. I took off my gloves, despite the cold, and leafed through them. There were instruction booklets and old bills, a few takeout menus. Most of the papers were swollen and stiff, but still legible. Some were frozen together.

And then, tucked between a Christmas card from a cousin and a drawing of a horse by Candace, there was a photograph.

The photo was curled and a bit stained, but otherwise pristine. In it, Shona and I stand side by side on the Painted Desert Trail, a wall of beautiful pink stone behind us, ochre dust beneath our feet. I am ducking somewhat, as though worried the camera—which I had propped up on a rock before setting the timer—would cut off my head. To my left, Shona is holding a bottle of water in her right hand, clutching it to her stomach. She is wearing denim shorts and a red T-shirt, sandals on her feet, and large, dark sunglasses on her face. I am on her right, wearing khaki shorts, a checked shirt, and sneakers. My left arm is over her shoulder. I have a kind of inadvertent smirk on my face. Shona is smiling.

When the photo was taken, I believed we wanted the same things. I believed we would have them. And I thought that was how we must have looked to the world, to anyone who cared to see: like a pair, matched, together. I thought anyone who looked at that photo would see the love and the heat coming off us like rays. But it was incomplete—like any photo is, I suppose—because it failed to show those things roiling and churning beneath the surface. Nor did it make visible those things beyond the frame, the countless, inconstant things broadcasting their signals to our too-susceptible hearts.

It hurt me, that cold morning amid the smouldering ashes, to look at that. We were two people who had made each other better for a short time. It's difficult not to mourn such a thing.

I held the picture between my fingers. Then I stood, walked back to the car, and tucked it into the glovebox. And then I drove away with Candace. I have never been back to that spot.

PHARAOHS

ANA RAE CAVERS squinted against the glare, fitted the toe of her right boot into the ski's binding, pressed down, and felt it click home. Then she did the same with her left.

The snow was only a few inches deep atop the lake. It had been a strange winter. She pushed out onto the ice, poling ahead, then gliding her feet after. The skiing was good across the surface, despite the strong wind whistling into her small bay through the pinched mouth that was bracketed by low, pine-topped rocks. She felt the cold carve right through her many layers of clothing. It was the coldest day of the winter to date. At midday it was still the temperature at which materials give up their characteristics and become hard, or brittle, cracking along heretofore invisible faults.

Her red skis created twin clefts in the perfect, clean snow. She leaned forward, her shoulders twinging on the odd pull-stroke. It took tremendous effort, but every so often the glide was right, and she moved as though a hand took her by the scruff of the neck and pulled her along, releasing her from all struggle and obligation.

Her face was pale and bloodless in that ungodly cold, her eyes like faint blue marbles in saucers of milk. Ice clung to her upper lip and coated her eyelashes, though she began to feel, as she skied on, a dampness in her grey hair and down her strong back from the exertion required to keep moving.

Ski trails criss-crossed the ice, but she seldom saw other skiers. Their tracks were like evidence of another civilization. Sometimes they lingered for days; other times a mean wind erased them nearly as quickly as they were put down. The tracks were cut every so often by the patterns left by snowmobiles, their twin front skis and rear central tracks. She saw the snowmobiles sometimes, too, great bands of them on weekends, ripping across the ice, making their throaty and whiny noise, kicking up clouds of snow. There were none today. It was a Tuesday.

Her twin sister, Sabina, was at that moment down in Florida, as she was every November through April. Ana Rae drove down every few years and enjoyed the break, but she didn't see how her enjoyment could do anything but diminish if she were to stay longer. Sabina—whose blond hair was, to a stranger, the only thing to distinguish her from Ana Rae—didn't see it that way. She hated winter and suggested every year that Ana Rae stay with her in Sarasota until the snow was gone.

But though the cold cracked the skin of her fingers, causing a searing pain when she plunged her hands into hot dishwater, and though the darkness felt at times interminable, Ana Rae knew she'd never give up her winters. They were so harshly beautiful, and somehow necessary to her sense of herself. The specific comfort of sitting by the woodstove with a glass of Chilean wine and a new book to read was not, she felt, duplicable in Florida.

The house where she lived those winters, as well as the humid, buggy summers, was barely a house at all. It was a cabin, a cottage. She and Jack had built it twenty-five years ago, shared it for only a few before he was gone. It began as a shack, twelve by twelve, with a roof and not much more. They'd added to it as they could afford the materials to do so, but even now, in its finished state, it lacked air conditioning, central heating, and running water in the winter. Every November she shut down the pump, hauled the foot valve from the lake, and poured antifreeze down the drains.

For most purposes she'd be on bottled water until May, though she kept an old white enamel pot on the woodstove and added handfuls of snow to it as it melted down. This she used to wash her dishes.

They'd done their best to insulate the house, though it had resisted their efforts. Frost furred certain spots on the floor, around doors, beneath the kitchen counter. The stove burned all winter, and she had a half-dozen little radiant parabolic heaters spaced throughout the place, including one on either side of the bed. There were a couple she had to be careful not to run at the same time or she'd blow a fuse, so she went from room to room turning them on and off as she moved through her day. There was another heater in the outhouse, strung off a fifty-foot extension cord. She used to let it run all the time, until she got sick of what it did to her electric bills; after that, she adopted the habit of plugging in the end of the cord, letting it heat up the small plywood box of an outhouse a few minutes before she would head out and down the little path. It didn't stop the cold from reaching up the hole, of course, but it was bearable. Anything is, if you're used to it.

She put up with all this because she valued nothing so highly as the silence the place afforded her. Her nearest neighbours, resident only on summer weekends, were on the far side of the bay, two hundred yards across the water and obscured by jack pines growing on a pair of tiny islands. The fire route on which she lived snaked by on the landward side, behind a hunk of Canadian Shield granite that more or less blocked the sound of the few vehicles which used the road. Most of what she heard all day was noise of her own making, or the birds in the oaks and pines surrounding the house, or the small ticking of the stove. She sometimes listened to the CBC on the transistor, for news and weather.

Ana Rae considered herself lucky to have made a life which so suited her desire to be alone. She missed Jack, of course, but knew that what she actually missed was a time in her life when they'd shared the project of life-building, and more things had seemed possible.

The ice—ten inches thick at least; she'd checked yesterday with the auger—settled invisibly, moving against itself, popping and groaning as it did so. It sounded at times like a penny dropped on a drumhead, other times like a plucked bass string, the dying reverberations of which could be felt in the feet. She was out on the open lake now, and its flatness spread out from her in every direction.

He had hit her, once. The children were still young. Afterwards, nothing was outwardly different. Inside everything had changed.

Out in the unobstructed wind there were patches of ice scoured clean of snow, windows down into the black water beneath, reminders that this was not simply flat ground. She passed the spot where she liked to swim in the summer, a small island of little more than rock and a few trees, with a stone ledge off of which she could dive into water that was forty feet deep. She'd last swum there in September, and it would likely be June before she could do it again.

After Jack was gone, others—Sabina, friends—kept putting men in her path, insisting she give them a chance. And there had been a man, just one. She and this man met several times, found each other's company tolerable, and eventually fumbled toward a single, unpleasant sexual encounter, after which they simply didn't speak again. It seemed to her, even at the time, like a mistake. It simply didn't feel right. It didn't feel like a part of her own life.

She sought nothing actively now, but saw how it was periodically necessary to pull in the nets she'd long ago set and suss out what she'd caught. Which was why she was headed across the ice now, to the far shore, to meet another man. As content as she was in her hermitage, she retained some stubborn residue of that girl's upbringing which taught her that her value lay in the willingness of men to pay attention to her. One did, so she was making her way toward him.

The thought of it seeped into a place directly between her shoulders, rode there on a blast of cold wind, and she hated the effort she was making. She could turn around now and invent some barrier to her visit, but she hated that thought, too. Straight-ahead in all things was how she meant to live now. To shear off all trite and sly exchanges. She would keep the appointment, but cut it short. One cup of tea, then back on her skis. That suited her, or nearly did anyway.

Richard, the man she was meeting, had bought a four-season place on the main road last summer. She'd run into him several times at the grocery store and three times out on the ice, skiing. He'd persisted with invitations, and now she was relenting. He seemed fine. Anyway, he apparently liked winter. She favoured hardy people, capable, sensible, and she thought he might prove to be some of those things.

Richard's house was on a point on the northwestern shore of the lake. From her house, in its shallow and tucked-away bay on the eastern edge, she could not see the spot. Once out on the open lake, though, it would come into view, low against the great concave sky and all the airy blue emptiness held there.

He would want to talk about their respective children. It was always the first topic, the thing that could be counted upon, the most obvious thing they had in common. She was not excited for this. It would feel to her like a desultory obligation, a shabby and half-hearted thing. Her children were like strangers to her now. She loved them, of course, and wished them well, but she observed them in their adult lives like they were characters on a television show. She was, quite honestly, only mildly curious about the details of their lives.

She could be honest with him and tell him that what she remembered most viscerally of her early motherhood was the loneliness, the suddenness and violence of her decentring, the guilt which attended it. Sitting in waiting rooms or on buses or walking grocery store aisles, aware that she'd gone from being herself to being this child's mother. How small it had made her feel. Ana Rae was cognizant, when raising her children, that much of her effort would come to nothing, and sometimes that knowledge brought out a panic or desperation she could barely contain. She just had to hold on until they could go off on their own, invent themselves—needed mostly just to feed and care for them. The rest happened, or it didn't.

Samantha was their first, when Jack was still substitute teaching. She was a confident, sprightly child who had to be chased. Ana Rae was exhausted, always. Then, eighteen months later, after Jack had found full-time work in a middle school, came Stephen. He was a needy and fragile, emotionally voracious child. As an adult, he still fit those descriptions.

When Jack died, the children were already in their twenties and, after some false starts, off on their own for good. At that point, being alone was no longer something Ana Rae could choose —it was the only way her life would be, unless she endeavoured by some brave orchestration to change it. But she did not wish to.

The house was still new then, and she spread out in it and took it as her shell. She spent the summers swimming and the autumns cutting wood, the winters skiing out on the ice, listening for signs that the lake was about to open up and swallow her. Ana Rae felt herself coming into her own with that new openness, that space all to herself. She was returning to the centre. Her life felt like something she had lent away so long ago that she'd forgotten about it, until it was given back to her. She found she'd missed it terribly.

When Ana Rae reached shore, she poked her bindings with the tips of her poles and stepped off her skis. Richard's house offered a flat wall of glass to the lake, high up, looking down; he stood at a window, waving to her. She stuck her skis in a mound of snow, her poles next to them, and started up toward the door. He opened it, said hello in a clear, sweet voice.

Richard was dressed in a finely combed cardigan, old jeans, and tasselled slippers, and he had a full head of silver hair which swooped up away from his face. He was handsome, and he knew it. The net result placed him at a deficit. His vanity was instantly obvious. She didn't know how she'd missed it when they'd met earlier. It was on his face. His hands were soft.

"Come in, come in," he said, ushering her into the entranceway of his large home. The central heat belched from vents all around her. An enormous stone fireplace stood at the far end of the room, unused. She unlaced her ski boots, shed her layers—hat, gloves, neck warmer, coat, snow pants—and placed them on a padded bench.

Beneath, she was damp and ruddy from the trip over. The feeling came back into her toes painfully.

"What a day. Coldest this year, I think," he said.

"I believe it is," she said.

"You could have cancelled. You must be frozen."

"I'm fine. Been here long enough to know how to dress for the cold."

"Of course," he said. He strode up three steps and into the kitchen, which looked down over the sunken living area and the bank of south-facing windows beyond, and placed a kettle on the range. "Come and sit," he said, and stretched out his arm, the end of which gestured to an overstuffed sofa.

She perched, cross-legged, her right knee pointed at him in a bid to discourage proximity. *You could have cancelled*, he'd said. *The cold.*

"I'm glad you came," he said. He was the only thing she'd seen move that day other than a large pileated woodpecker on a dead oak by her shoreline. He moved elaborately, showily. He spoke with his hands, and his face was comically expressive.

She recognized the dance. The dance had not changed.

Before Jack hit her that once—sober, so it hurt more— she'd thought him nearly perfect. He was far from it, but it took a while to learn that. At best, he was closer to perfect than ninety-nine percent of them. But that still left far too much room. Attractive men—by which she meant handsome, capable, not stupid, kind, selfless—were exceedingly rare. Lightning struck with greater reliability. The rest were silly, their motives embarrassingly transparent.

"Tell me about your children," Richard said, on cue. The kettle began to sing. He stood and danced up the three steps to remove it from the heat.

"They're grown," she said.

"Yes, so are mine. Do you hear from them often?"

"Often enough." She checked her email once a week at the small public library in town, and usually there was a note or two from her children, which she dutifully answered. There were phone calls around birthdays and holidays, too, and to her mind that was enough. She saw the angle from which such thinking appeared uncharitable, but she'd long ago stopped caring about such angles and gave no effort to meet them.

After she and Jack had finished the house, they set about building a garage, closer to the road, next to the granite outcropping. A place to store fishing rods and tools and cans of motor oil, and stow the twelve-foot aluminum boat in the winter. When they were done putting it up, they stood inside looking at the uninsulated ceiling and exposed beams, and Jack said, *Those are suicide rafters*. She did not laugh with him. Having so recently come back to herself, she felt it in terribly poor taste to even discuss such wilful violence to one's own person. She held that comment against Jack until he died.

Seated in his light pine-panelled sunken living space, Richard offered her many such opportunities for resentment. He was generous with them. The one she found most difficult to let go came when he returned with her mug of tea, set it down in front of her, and said, "Don't you feel you owe them everything? That they're the reason you're here?"

"I think it's the other way around, if you want to be literal," she said, and then laughed at herself.

"Well," he said, "different ways of looking at the same thing, I guess."

She was bored with the subject, so she started looking around the place. Her eye fell on a great many things, none of which interested her. Richard watched her looking, waiting for something to catch her attention.

"I just had that Rolling Stones poster framed," he said.

"Isn't that something."

"I saw them in Rome once. Incredible."

"Isn't that something," she said.

"That photo was taken on Bondi Beach in Australia," he said, indicating a framed portrait of himself in small red trunks and a big straw hat. "Have you ever been?"

"Never."

"Gorgeous spot."

"I'm sure."

"In six weeks in Australia I don't think I once put on a shirt," he said, and laughed. There seemed to be an offer of something; he behaved as though it was obvious, understood, like he held at the end of his arm a meaning she need only reach out to grasp. It seemed to have something to do with sex. No, the dance hadn't changed.

She thought, *You ridiculous man. Your worldliness is a thin veneer.*

"That was a wonderful trip. We took four months just to go where we pleased. We'd just put the kids in university and were feeling a bit at loose ends. That was a year before we divorced, Diane and I."

"I'm sorry."

"No, it was perfect. We sort of found who we were. I think I had my moment on that trip. After Australia we flew to Egypt. At Giza I found myself thinking, look at what these people built! What am I doing?"

"Humbling," she said.

"Incredibly. Of course, there are no more pharaohs. Long gone."

"No. And that's too bad."

"Have you travelled much?"

"On a teacher's pension and his tiny life insurance? No. This is my travel. Skiing across the lake. Sometimes I visit my sister in Florida."

"You seem like someone who would love it. You have a curiosity about you."

"I satisfy it in books. They're what I've got."

Ana Rae was at times prone to a kind of insidious inertia. That was the only way she could explain why she hadn't already left Richard's house. Hardy as she was, it *was* damned cold out on that lake, and his couch, which she now settled into with her legs folded beneath her, *was* comfortable. He offered a second cup of tea, and she accepted. Richard was full of faults, but it was nice to converse with someone every now and then. Most of that winter she'd heard only her own voice.

The sun was sinking, cold and brilliant, over the edge of the lake. Winter afternoons disappeared so quickly.

Richard said, "I should think about making you dinner. What do you say?"

"Thanks, but I have a soup going in the slow cooker. It'll burn or go to waste if I leave it."

"Nibblies, then. You'll need your strength to get back across that lake." He swept up the steps again and set about putting together a cheese tray, crackers, grapes. In a few moments he returned with it and placed it on the coffee table near her knees. She grazed at it a while, as the light coming in the windows went a deep blue, then black, and she found herself looking at her own reflection, and that of Richard, sitting at the other end of his overstuffed sofa.

"Diane used to say of this time of day, in the winter, that the day left before it even arrived. It feels that way sometimes, doesn't it."

"I love the suddenness of it. Day, then whoop, here's night. No pleasantries."

"That's a funny way of looking at it."

She'd expected there would come a point, a comment or a disagreement, that would force the end of her meeting with Richard, and indeed possibly even of their friendship, or whatever it could be called. Something remarkable, a gaffe or conflict to redraw the lines, or erase them altogether. But the afternoon had passed without such a thing happening. That was partly due to Richard's accommodating way. He seemed to refuse to be bothered, bending this way and that to roll with the frequent stops and redirections she inserted into their conversation. His smile—courteous, deferential, the soft lips turned up at the corners like quotation marks—was the same now as when she'd arrived. Only the light had changed.

"My skis must be frozen," she said. "They'll snap in half if I'm not careful."

"You're going to leave now, aren't you? That's too bad."

"It's dark. I should get home."

"I hope we can do this again."

"Thank you for the tea," she said.

Ana Rae reapplied the layers and accessories meant to keep her warm beneath the invisible dome of Arctic air. Outside, the night was sharp and cruel. A dazzling half moon looking down onto the snow and the ice.

He'd hit her with an open hand, flush across the cheek.

There'd been no warning. They'd argued before in just the same way, but he'd never even feigned violence. Then that. Afterwards he'd said nothing, just gone away. She heard the car starting and he drove off. Later he said he'd just gone around in circles, nowhere in particular. He behaved as though he himself were wounded.

She stepped back into her bindings, put her gloved hands through the loops atop her poles, and then she pushed off onto the ice. It was silver beneath the moon. Everything was clearer in that deep cold, as though the lid had been lifted off the world, letting all the stars in, all the moon's brilliance, inviting all the universe's unfathomable cold to pour down over her.

Below her feet was ice, and beneath the ice, forty or sixty or a hundred feet down, atop billion-year-old granite, there lay a darkness of a totality she could not imagine. Ten inches of frozen water lay between her and it.

She pulled and glided, finding her tracks from the trip over earlier that day. She would ski for twenty minutes more, and then she would stoke or relight the fire before finding something to eat. There was no soup waiting. The moon shone down indifferently, and the wind was still. She entered between the rocks at the mouth of her bay, where nothing stirred. She came to the end of her own tracks and unfastened the skis' bindings, looking up at the shape of her house, dark amid the trees, and small, and empty, thank God, wholly empty.

LANDS AND FORESTS

WHEN HE WAS twenty-six years old, Frank MacDougall watched a fire consume the town of Haileybury in a matter of hours.

It was October. With the fire season passed, the rangers had already been sent home, though everything was still dry as tinder. When the wind came up, it fanned the farmers' burn piles into great hungry flames which moved on the town as fast as an automobile and climbed two hundred feet up into the air.

As the whole town was going up, MacDougall was standing up to his chin in the water of Lake Temiskaming, a sodden blanket over his head. He was among maybe two or three dozen other people similarly huddled, their heads just above the water's surface, the curling heat on their faces, their bodies rigid in the cold lake. With his boot, he poured water over the blankets of those near him to keep them from catching if touched by embers or falling debris. There were mothers with children. An elderly wife and husband, their faces frozen in rictuses of age and grief. Labourers and shopkeepers. Struck dumb, all of them, by the sight before them. The children cried. MacDougall's bones sang with pain and he could not feel his fingers or toes.

Above the roaring of combustion, he could hear the trees' piercing shrieks as the gases and resin and water contained within them came to an instant boil, building pressure until they forced their way out the way vapour escapes a whistling tea kettle. Each sound would be followed by a pop and a rushing as the fuel—leaves, needles, bark, branches—erupted into flame.

It was fantastic and horrific. The choking smell of hot resin and smoke and scorched lumber and superheated stone, the hiss of embers falling into the water, the red pall thrown over everything he could see, the sky gone orange at midnight, the magnitude of it. The awareness that nothing could be done to stop it.

He harboured a clarity, as he stood in the black water and watched everything turn to ash, that if he were to survive, the moment would persist for him, would continue to prove remarkable as the decades unfurled. It stood even above such moments as kissing Pearl for the first time, her skin fragrant and her lips soft as kid leather, or taking a Belgian hilltop from the Kaiser's Sixth Army, the gas scraping his eyes and scoring his lungs.

When the body of the fire finally moved on, to the unbroken forest beyond, it left behind nothing but isolated spots of flame, the fallen beams of homes and shops crackling like campfire. The next day, rain came and then turned to snow, flakes sizzling as they landed, useless individually, but in aggregate working to extinguish what still burned.

It was there that MacDougall realized he was bound to a life shaped by fire.

The next ten years brought births, advancements, setbacks, the intimation of middle age's approaching tranquility— but they did not deliver him any sense of mastery over fire's dominion. He had left Haileybury with a firm resolve in his breast, and it took him to Sault Ste. Marie, where the air service was headquartered, and where they put him in the open cockpit of a bright yellow Fairchild KR-34. That resolve carried him airborne, got him deeply involved in the great project to harness flight for the detection and management of fire.

He would joke, too, that being in the air beat being on the ground because there are no blackflies at two thousand feet.

In September of 1931 he sped out over the river's brassy funnel toward Michigan, the wind in his mouth, before dipping a wing and banking around, doubling back toward the southeast to cruise over the rock and low tree cover of Algoma, gaining the French River as it spread and split and split again at its delta. The edges of Georgian Bay glinted silver, giving way to a cloudy tan, then a deep blue, before going green-black. Sudbury thereafter, and in its downwind lea the fantail of black smelter fog. Finally the lush arboreal carpet thickening as he came over Algonquin Park, of which he'd been named superintendent. If, as Saint-Exupéry posited, the airplane revealed the true face of the earth, the Superintendent was looking for signs of worry on that face.

The late-summer warmth had broken the day before and the temperature had dropped precipitously to just above freezing. It was ten degrees colder in the air. At the Fairchild's controls he sat wrapped in a winter flight suit, fur-lined—even the goggles, where they met his face, trimmed in beaver—with gloves the length of his arms, all of it worn over a layer of wool. Still, despite the thin sweat over his entire body, the cold reached him.

He was five hundred feet over Cache Lake. A fine spray of oil from the engine coated the glass of his goggles, caught in the slipstream and flowing over the aircraft's windshield. Every few minutes he lifted a hand to wipe it away with the back of a glove.

The Superintendent put down in the lake and motored in to dock at the lodge there. He received a report and some supplies, then took off again and steered north, toward Burntroot Lake, where he had been told poachers were present and at work. In most cases, the cough and sputter of the Wright radial engine coming in low over the treetops was enough to dissuade men from unsanctioned pursuit of moose meat, or from haunting others' traplines, but it was occasionally required of him to land the aircraft and intercept the hunters with an impromptu face to face.

The unlimited ceiling accepted him. Wind howled through the empty seat, tucked beneath the upper wing, in front of him. His aircraft was nakedly practical, a shoebox with wings. Nothing extraneous. There was very little between the seat of his flight suit and the empty air, and the ground below that. Just lacquered fabric stretched over a wooden skeleton, some wire, a bit of glass, all of it pulled along by the hammering radial engine up front, its prop cutting the air to ribbons. He flew, he was aware, ever proximate to his own death.

In addition to the reported poachers, an island on Big Trout had been lit by a lightning strike three days earlier. He would drop in there, after reconnoitring Burntroot, to check in on the crew he'd dispatched to cut a line and weaken the blaze before it leapt the narrow passage and began feeding on the vast green expanse beyond.

The meaning of landscape varies by viewer, and the Superintendent suspected that it acted as moral mirror. Levelling off at a thousand feet, what he saw was, to him, something to inspire love, but which was itself indifferent to it. Rich late-day sunlight falling on deep emerald terrain pocked everywhere by the copper gleam of lakes and rivers.

The open places in the marshes, where even now he could see moose feeding, three of them, up to their haunches in the tannin-rich muck.

The Superintendent had also seen the fields of the Western Front, ones denuded and blackened by ordnance and gas. The latter had done a number on his lungs and was a fairly direct cause of his having chosen an outdoor line of work. It was tempting to see cause and effect throughout that sequence. His working his way into the life he would eventually know, in order to offer, on behalf of the Department of Lands and Forests, some amends to Nature—however insignificant those amends, and however distant from the War.

Things tend not to be that clean, though, and nothing remains pristine.

Pretty as Algonquin was, they'd long ago taken all the original white pine out of it, or all that was worth cutting anyway. Two-hundred-and-fifty-foot monsters knocked down and hauled over ice and taken by train to mills, or intact aboard ships, to be made into ships themselves. Any orphans left standing were lopsided or bent and couldn't be used. They'd stand until they fell over or fire took them.

The world was heaving, convulsing into some new shape. He felt it with the same sense that told him when fire was imminent, told him when the tall trees, their tops wavering in the troubled air, were due to flare. He understood that old certainties were dead—that we live in an approximation, a rough convergence of crooked lines, a messy agglomeration of elements made in order to be unmade and remade, cohering only just enough that we might recognize pattern and call it a world.

He was aware that the majority of those who came to places like this one visited them as they might historic battlefields or the resting spots of martyrs. They came to see where nature had once happened but was happening no more. All the frontiers were falling or had fallen. Forestmen now spoke in terms more scientific than descriptive. Language was changing, and with it, the way people thought.

Still he retained a belief that such change could be negotiated. That these hot, oily, metallic machines, their motors low-sounding and esophageal, could be harnessed to positive effect. That his aircraft was an instrument for detecting fire, and that other craft would one day aid in dousing it. His radio granted him the ability to signal fire's presence to others—to summon, to warn. Planes, trucks, and canoes bringing crews to where they could fight it.

He believed, with all this, that humans might yet prove to be of some benefit.

The sky was riddled with crags and pockets which couldn't be seen, only felt in judders and dips. The Superintendent set his aim north. In ten minutes, he descended to just under three hundred feet and circled over Burntroot, looking for signs of men, their gear and belongings, their rifles. He saw, within a ring of ramrod straight black spruce, a clearing with the remnants of a cooking fire but no equipment. He saw boot prints on the loamy shore but no people. They'd moved on, and he'd missed them.

He tracked back to the south. It was only a short flight before Big Trout appeared through a bluish haze, more like a memory of a place than a place itself. The water of the lake was the same colour as the sky: washed blue fading to pink at its edges, with a tawdry swipe of orange at its rim, the reflected glow of the heat of the fire, the object of his crews' efforts.

The Superintendent descended again, dropping in low over a sandy ridge which itself dropped into a wetland. He put down where the water opened up, with the island to his left, and after riding the wave of his own wake, steered the plane across the shallow lake toward the western tip and the firefighters' camp. There, he was received by a pair of men who'd been tending pots, cooking supper for the dozen men still off in the island's interior. There was no dock at the camp, so George Flynn—in stiff olive trousers, Wellingtons, and an undershirt, a bright red chigger rash on his forearms—waded out into the water to catch the KR-34's float and steer it toward shore, where the Superintendent tossed a rope to the other man, John Ferguson, who tied it to the trunk of a tamarack near where the firemen had landed their canoes.

The Superintendent, stiff in his thick flight suit, climbed down from the cockpit and stood on the float. "Boys," he said, "how are things here?"

"Not so bad, sir," said Ferguson. "They're saying they've got it out but for some spots and the smouldering. Boys are out turning over the hot spots and spraying them, but I think that'll be it."

"Good," said the Superintendent. "You'll come in tomorrow, then?"

"That's the thinking," said Flynn.

"Great work, lads. Just great."

"Weren't much of a fire," said Ferguson. "Schoolgirls could've put it out."

Once they confirmed it was extinguished, there would come the labour of carrying out the hundred-and-fifty-pound pump, the linen hoses with their brass couplings laid out to dry in the sun and the air and then coiled into sacks to be ready for the next fire, whether the next week or the next year. The dozen or so men would then pack up their tents and grub boxes, jerry cans and tool boxes and lubricants, their axes, shovels, McLeod and Pulaski tools, and return to the lodgings at Cache Lake. There, they would wonder if it was the season's last fire, and if so, when they'd be released to the other half of their year. Released, to scare up ad hoc winter employment in cities or in small towns, Elliot Lake or Saginaw or Ottawa. Back to their dark days of vagrancy, alcohol, despondency, the women they hoped were still there. Only the Superintendent and a skeleton crew of a few others would remain, including his mechanic, Landon Steeves, who would soon be required to help swap out the Fairchild's floats for skis.

The seasons moved the men around as though they were wildlife, driven by need across the map from one circumstance to another, their brotherhood temporary but their instinct for survival unwavering.

In time, they took him out of the bush, named him Deputy Minister, and gave him an office at Queen's Park. The biplane was long gone, but MacDougall could not prevent, from time to time, the geysering up of an uncontrollable desire to be in the forest.

After the second war, he handed a list to a design team at De Havilland and said, "Make a plane that meets each of these requirements and I'll buy twenty-five of them." The specs described what turned out to be the world's most reliable pickup truck, with wings. They called it the Beaver. The Provincial Air Service took delivery in 1948, replacing their aging Stinsons and Norsemans, and thereafter used the Beaver to patrol, supply, ferry, rescue.

One was set aside for the personal use of the Deputy Minister, stationed at Toronto. He could be in the air with an hour's notice, when he felt that geysering desire, when fire season hit its stride, when he wanted to see how things were progressing, when he wanted out of the city.

At the end of a tremendously dry summer, the island on Big Trout was again ignited by lightning—only this time, the blaze had leapt the narrow passage and raced to meet a second blaze, product of an unextinguished campfire, which had begun farther to the north and west. The two fires were drawn together as though magnetic.

He was told that a fire crew had lost a radio, and that the replacement needed to be flown out from the Sault. Feeling acutely the longing for action, he radioed and said he'd fly up that afternoon to make the delivery, and to help coordinate at the park if necessary, to lift morale.

He flew the yellow Beaver at five hundred feet through air thick with pollen, yellow-green clouds of it in the smoky false dusk, bluish-grey. Columns of soft summer air braided together with fire-heated gusts, on which rode delicate embers which zipped by the Beaver's windshield as he aimed at the flaming horizon.

Unlike fire, whose sole governing principle is consumption, flight is a bargain with an unreliable friend. A hot wind hit his tail and knocked the plane sideways and downward, the stick jumping to life in the Deputy Minister's hand.

For the slimmest instant, he thought he would be unable to correct his path before crashing broadside into a sheet of fire. Everything—the fire, the plane below him, the stick— possessed agency. Everything but him. In that instant, he had a desire to live, to last, but the difference between desire and agency was quite clear to him just then, as was the idea that he'd ultimately been in control of so little, propelled by a mysterious driver, a Protestant uneasiness coupled with harrowing experience that flung him, again and again, into the path of catastrophe. But it was only for an instant.

At last report, the firemen had dug and fought and cut their way to a wide country where the soil atop the bedrock was thin and tree cover was sparse, a perfect firebreak to transect the fire's advance. He'd known this corner of the park well, as he had most all of its corners, but in the wake of the fire it appeared completely foreign to him.

Such mutability always moved him to speechlessness. His heart would go membranous, feeling as though it might disintegrate altogether right there in his chest. How amazing and deadly and unpredictable, fire's supple advances and retreats, its crooked lines, moving as though on the balls of its feet, always a risk to wriggle and shirk its way from constraint to freedom.

Beauty does not require us, thought the Deputy Minister. *It does not bend to our avowals or beliefs. It will outlast us. It will forget we were ever here.*

To the north, the afternoon was already as dark as night. He flew straight toward it. Creeping fires consumed mosses and duff and slash, while crown fires jumped the tops of two-hundred-foot-tall conifers, candling—it was aptly called—trees like matches, their heads popping into brilliant light. Where the fire had already left its imprint, the acres smouldered. The ash there would fold under and next year the new growth would begin.

Elsewhere, engineers and foresters were at work developing ways to drop great quantities of water from the sky, arranging a new marriage of man and machine in the service of nature.

Elsewhere, Pearl sat alone.

Elsewhere, forests were not burning, but were damp and heavy with frequent rain, and families were camping beneath rich green canopies and breathing in the fragrant, resinous air, and men taught their sons to shoot deer with heirloom Remingtons.

And elsewhere, farther to the north, beyond that wall of flame, were the places where sturdy and foolhardy people had, a century earlier, attempted to cut a life from the great, thick forest. Where forgotten gravestones deep in the brush and tangle waited to be uncovered and burned clean.

Back at the park, campers and rangers would report being overrun with wolves and coyotes, alive in the daylight, fleeing in advance of the fire. Owls flying thick as June dragonflies. All the trains through the park's southern corridor had been cancelled.

The Deputy Minister flew low enough now for the top of a burning Scots pine, detached and caught in a draft, to brush his left pontoon. It woke him up, here in the vivid and perilous heart of things. He belonged nowhere else.

He descended and steadied the Beaver, landed on the sediment-draped surface of Big Trout, and cruised toward the beach, where tents had been erected. There he was met by men he did not know, men with red faces and necks tarnished by the sun, bulging forearms, the knees of their trousers worn thin. They unloaded the radio and some instruments, and beneath their greetings and utterances there lingered some slight awe for the Deputy Minister, a legend here in their presence, flesh and bone. He and all his accomplishments, and his undiminished sensitivity to factors both airborne and subterranean.

Time was slow and hallucinatory. Casual conversations took place a hundred yards from the maw of a raging wildfire. The sun-heated pine needles beneath their feet wove into the scent of the fire, the fire which could also be heard, its heat felt in addition to that of the sun. In the dogwoods and cedars at the island's edge there were chattering squirrels which either did not care about the fire or recognized their inability to escape it and so carried on, and would do so right up until the moment they were incinerated. Not far away, silent in its determined, prehistoric movements, a snapping turtle the size of a Buick's hubcap walked out from beneath a juniper bush, slid into the water, suddenly graceful, and was gone.

The weather changed. In the end, that's what it really took. The pumps and hoses, the firebreaks—they were all just meant to slow the fires, to hold them in place, until the weather changed.

A thickness in the air and then a drenching rain. Two days of it, leaving the ground black and smouldering, pricked with the charcoal skeletons of trees.

If only we could be the weather, thought the Deputy Minister.

At Cache Lake, the men cleaned off in the dormitory showers. Steam poured from the windows. Later, they sat outdoors while the sun sank over the tops of the trees and loons called. The day's exertions settled in their limbs, making them heavy as cast concrete. They reclined in low chairs and let the dusk settle over their bodies. The mosquitoes, midges, and cluster flies came then, and the men swatted them casually, ineffectually, a gesture of habit, though their roughened limbs felt nothing in those moments save the sweet static of inactivity. Later they moved indoors, and drank beer and stared into the great iron stove, at knuckle-sized coals of glowing red.

The Deputy Minister led them through it all, in conversation and in music. Among his things, regardless of where he went, was a scuffed and worn leather case, within which nested a violin he'd made himself from a hunk of maple pulled from the park. It was warm and beautiful, and from it he was able to coax everything in the world, each sound, from joy and comradeship to sorrow, an almost Balkan misery. By now he knew each man's name, and told jokes to all of them, walking among them, weaving them together, this large man, larger for his comfort and exuberance, his neck like twisted oak, arms and chest on a scale which might best be described in automotive terms.

He wore green worsted serge trousers, a khaki shirt rolled to the elbows, unbuttoned to midchest in the heat to reveal the undershirt, and boots which came high up his shins, their leather creased and puckered, indented at the eyelets, with the sort of character you'd find on the face of a person in the perfect moment of their life. The Deputy Minister wasn't ignorant to fashion—he simply lived outside its jurisdiction.

Finally, when none of the men remained in the common room, he retired to his old superintendent's cabin, a short, dewy walk across a clearing, and found there his bedroll. He blew out his lamp and fell instantly to sleep. The next morning, he woke with the first birds, and walked in his undershirt and trousers and unlaced boots over to the dormitory's mess, where he sang while he cooked for the men. Then, when the last pan was scrubbed, he put his things aboard the Beaver and rose, the water dripping off his pontoons, motor singing, banking toward the south and back to the west. To Toronto, bright and noisome, and to all it held.

Then MacDougall was sixty-seven years old. He sat in a dark suit and freshly polished brogues, his hands in his lap, at a table in a ballroom in Toronto. He was attempting to focus on the words of the event's host, but his thoughts wandered. He shifted uneasily. He was not yet retired, yet they were lauding him, in terms he associated with someone who had nothing left to accomplish.

When news of the impending honour had found him, it was accompanied by a tremendous discomfort at the thought of being the focus of such attention, as well as an irksome disquiet at the prospect of giving a speech to a room full of people. He'd rather tell a joke and then his play violin. Would they let him do that? Talking about himself wasn't a thing he particularly liked doing. He was beside the point. There were more important things, practical things as well as tender things.

He'd wanted a full life, while life was his, and to raise and send forth healthy and happy children. Every day, he felt in his body—among the few uncomplicated and uncompromised things within him—the clean, smokeless combustion of his love for them. But over that he had only so much control. He and Pearl had had three children, and he had outlived two of them.

The park, though, and the wild places—the trees, the coyotes cleaning deer carcasses, blue asters on the forest floor, the fragility of shadows in moonlight on snow—might yet stand close to forever. Available to all, but owned by none.

"He is renowned for his practical development of aircraft modifications and utilization and the protection of forested areas and wilderness parks," said the host at the dais, but the Deputy Minister lost the rest to a ringing sound in his ears, the cumulative residue of a lifetime of propellers and cylinders, which faded into a low hum as his attention drifted.

Life was not equally measured. There were small instances within which more living was done than in other, greater stretches of time. Much of his life had occurred in those condensed moments: ones in which he'd encountered a will greater than his own, a faceless will. Though he knew it was advisable not to see such moments as personal confrontations, he knew also that he was humbled in them.

Somehow, he had survived. Come out of each such experience with his life. Here he was. He'd been alongside good people. Had flown with some of them over a great forest as, below, the flora became heat and light. He'd stood in a lake with the freezing water up to his neck and watched the trees immediately beyond the town fall like a curtain to reveal the land rising beyond, to the north and west. Watched the inferno expanding in all directions, its scale and power revealing to him, with great clarity, the awful enormity of the world.

ACKNOWLEDGEMENTS

I'd like to acknowledge and thank the Ontario Arts Council for a generous grant in support of this book.

I'm grateful to the editors of *Maisonneuve* for shaping, improving, and publishing "Emmylou" in their Winter 2017 issue.

Thanks to those who read and helped with early versions of these stories or this manuscript, especially Eric Fershtman, Seyward Goodhand, and Rick Taylor.

I'm indebted to several publications, including *Sylva: The Lands and Forests Review*, published by the government of Ontario from 1945–61, and *Trees of Ontario* by Linda Kershaw. For information and direction, thanks also to Todd Fleet and the staff of the Canadian Bushplane Heritage Centre in Sault Ste. Marie, Ontario, and to Michelle Curran and Scott Nichols of the Peterborough Multi-Sport Club.

If this book possesses any redeeming qualities whatsoever, they are the result of the efforts of Bryan Jay Ibeas, an extraordinary editor and a wonderful friend, with whom I have long wanted to work on such a project, and finally had the chance to do so. I hope there are more such opportunities in the future.

For company and support on adventures which fuelled many of these stories, thanks are due to Alice Winchester and John Dungavell.

I'm grateful to Leigh Nash and the entire Invisible team for their continued belief in my work.

Love and thanks to Denee and Gordon Forbes, to Sharron and John Curley, to Adelaide, Cormac, and Theo, and to the rest of my family, spread coast to coast. I'm sorry I haven't visited more.

And finally, thank you to Christie Curley, for inspiring this book, and for making it possible.

INVISIBLE PUBLISHING produces fine Canadian literature for those who enjoy such things. As a not-for-profit publisher, our work includes building communities that sustain and encourage engaging, literary, and current writing.

Invisible Publishing has been in operation for over a decade. We released our first fiction titles in the spring of 2007, and our catalogue has come to include works of graphic fiction and non-fiction, pop culture biographies, experimental poetry, and prose.

We are committed to publishing diverse voices and experiences. In acknowledging historical and systemic barriers, and the limits of our existing catalogue, we strongly encourage LGBTQ2SIA+, Indigenous, and writers of colour to submit their work.

Invisible Publishing is also home to the Bibliophonic series of music books and the Throwback series of CanLit reissues.

If you'd like to know more, please get in touch:
info@invisiblepublishing.com